Praise for Soft

Wonderful story-telling. Thi
takes you on a journey – the ~~past~~ ....
present. Powerful images, compelling and disturbing.
Intensely readable.

Alex Larson, *Personal Assistant*

The style and atmosphere are what grab you; there is
a sense of foreboding that draws you on a journey to a
place where guilt and innocence become inseparable.

Pat Lewis, *Retired Librarian*

A compassionate and heart-rending story of an ordinary
family coping with loss. Deeply moving, funny and
poignant.

Debbie Mann, *Case-coordinator*

Carly writes from the heart to the heart.

Karen Long, *Office Manager*

An obsessive, evocative, page-turning good read.

Sue Owen, *Artist*

A haunting tale, imaginatively told. Peppered with
belly-aching moments of laughter and pathos.

Trevor Curtis, *Registered Nurse*

The depiction of family life is so well described I forgot I
was reading fiction. Loved it.

Christina Deaken

Dearest Becks
enjoy!
xx

Soft Belly Days

Carly Nugent

love Tom
xx

MPress books

Soft Belly Days

First published in the United Kingdom in 2011 by MPress Books

Copyright © Carly Nugent 2011

MPress Books Limited Reg. No 6379441 is a company registered in Great Britain
www.mpressbooks.co.uk

British Library Cataloguing in Publication Data
A catalogue record for this book is available from the British Library.

Where possible, papers used by MPress Books are natural, recyclable products made from wood grown in sustainable forests. The manufacturing processes conform to the environmental regulations of the country of origin.

ISBN
978-0-9565077-0-9

Typeset in Palatino
Origination by Core Creative, Yeovil 01935 477453
Printed and bound in England by MPG Biddles Limited

Author's note

I have taken a few liberties with the landscape. There isn't a Tinner's Arms in Carn Brea village, and I moved St. Uny Churchyard so it was just an eight-minute run from South Crofty Mine. For this I apologise, and I wish no offence. (And I suspect someone could do it in eight minutes.)

Acknowledgements

I am deeply indebted to Brian, Lisa and Oscar Mortensen-Cave, Reg Jarvis, Glen Snow, Dr. John Singleton of Manchester Metropolitan University, and Colin Rodgers of The Cornwall Film Fund who have encouraged this book from its inception as a screenplay.

Also, a huge thanks to Iain Paterson for his unstinting support and who eloquently captured, in two sketches, the journey of Rachel.

Appreciation to Andrew Marshall and his team for their faith in this story.

To my family and friends without whom this would not have happened.

Finally, I have to thank Paddy and Eileen Nugent who were the inspiration for the characters Jack and Ruth.

Cover Illustration by Tomislav Tikulin.
www.tomtikulin-art.com

For my sister Debbie Nugent

Soft Belly Days

by Carly Nugent

In the silent mind lies the master of life, within this stillness its mysteries are revealed. Seek to be still and know who you are, for beguiled by emotions we are blind.

It's 3am. November cold and a little eerie without the squawking gulls. I take off my boots and socks and walk across Carbis Bay beach, sinking my feet into the cold, acquiescent sand. It is as fine as caster sugar, and as I lift my foot the sand momentarily wraps around my ankle, tightly holding on before reluctantly letting go.

In the distance, on the black rocks, Godrevy Lighthouse flashes like an indolent firefly. The waves break, white as soap suds, edging black velvet with intricate crochet, as they lift then spill, lift then spill.

I'm here tonight and have been here every night for the past six weeks because my father is dying. I come here, driven by helplessness, to appeal to the good nature of any god or angel prepared to listen to grant us more time. Hope, for me, has become one shooting star, one match struck in the heavens to assure me that my father is still invincible. I have a heart filled with hope.

My father's name is Jack. Jack Tangye. I am Rachel. This is our dance. This is our coming together and our parting.

And there is someone else. Someone else who keeps me from my warm bed and the wondrous anaesthetic of sleep: there is Abigail, Abigail Daylight.

I haven't thought about her for years, but lately I have caught her in my peripheral vision. Staring at me with those black eyes, those myopic black eyes, and I turn to confront her – as I never could as a child – but like a spectre she vanishes. Each time I'm left wondering if I've simply made her up.

As I stare out to sea I am paralysed by a feeling that somewhere, deep in the ocean, rests something in the sands which stirs in response to the tides and the more subtle currents which tease at its anchor and loosens its chains . . . and I wonder if I'm ready? If I'll ever be ready, for the wreckage that will come floating towards me? Spilling flotsam from my mind . . .

One

The Bus Journey

Abigail Daylight struggles through the bus; she has black shoulder-length hair that is beginning to whiten at the temples. The twisted and tangled hair reveals lice clinging to their hostess like nobody's at a somebody's party. Abigail has blackened blood beneath her fingernails where she has scratched at her scalp. Her dark eyes are enormous behind her thick lenses, glued into thick black frames: they're man's glasses. She wears a man's overcoat too, buttoned to the neck. The hem skims the floor, brushing aside flattened cigarette butts.

Abigail Daylight carries her emptiness with her, marked out with black ink upon blue Basildon Bond. These are her love letters to Johnny, and scrunched into soft paper balls they slope her shoulders with the weight of granite stones.

Abigail carries this load everywhere in carrier bags; two made from nylon and three made of paper, with handles of string.

Dearest Johnny,

There are things I need to tell you that I never said out loud. Things I should have said but the words became stuck somewhere between my heart and my head, like a crumb breathed in instead of swallowed.

I do not remember the moment when the ivy first entwined about my neck, choking the honeyed voice that whispered into first your right ear and then your left . . .

Abigail drifts backwards in her mind, an entire decade, to 1955, to the room of whitewashed walls, to a sumptuous satin quilt the colour that of a full-bodied Bordeaux.

Back to her lover's unfathomable brown eyes and his pale white skin, untouched by the sun.

Back to the room where she remembers the whisper, "Fill me up Johnny, fill me up." Back to where shadows play on the walls and the oil burns in the lamp and where, touched with his tongue, she is made beautiful.

Seated on the same bus is Rachel. Rachel is eight

years old and this is her first ever journey without an adult. She is nervous but not afraid.

She is a long way from the woman she'll become, the woman of her future, who strides across the frosted sands trying to accept her father's dying, trying to make sense of her past . . .

A frightened Rachel squirms in her seat, not quite believing who she has just seen. The short journey, barely a mile, from Redruth to Barncoose had gone better than she had dared hope. She has done all that her mother asked of her: got straight off at the main bus stop, walked quickly to the department store where she had handed over an envelope containing a small book and some money, and then patiently waited while the lady with bright red purse-string lips and scarlet fingernails had counted the notes and wrote in the book. This was an important task; it meant that they would be keeping their furniture. And Rachel had taken back the envelope, returned to the bus stop, and not once talked to a stranger.

Everything had happened exactly as her mother had told her it would, except that her mother hadn't mentioned that Abigail Daylight used the bus.

Abigail Daylight, the local bag lady. Abigail Daylight, the local witch. The local witch who cast spells and who cast them (according to her brothers anyway) on little girls. Just girls.

Abigail Daylight, who could take out your beating heart just by looking at you, used this bus.

On seeing Abigail, Rachel squeezes her eyes tightly shut and tries desperately to make the image disappear. For a brief moment she succeeds, opening her mind's eye to watch as the hem of a white robe worn by Jesus skims over rose petals and a woman so pale her skin is a translucent blue reaches forward and dares to touch this hem as it teases Jesus' sandalled toes. The woman at once blushes pink, and pearly tears slip over salted cheeks, quenching dry lips so that they may kiss once again. She smiles a tremulous smile and Jesus smiles and moves on.

However, it is not Jesus. It is Abigail. Rachel rushes towards the door and presses the STOP bell, a red rubber button. The conductor stands over her, spitting saliva through his long, grey, nicotine-stained moustache. "Touch that again and I'll chop your fingers off." Startled by this unfamiliar tone of voice Rachel steps backwards, straight into Abigail Daylight, where indeed, with just one look, Rachel's small beating heart shifts up inside of her, clogging her ever-tightening throat. For the first time in her life Rachel feels real fear. Not the scary anticipation of what her brothers might do to her next – she knew her father would always take her side over them, and just their knowing that always saved her – but something different, something visceral. This was an acute aliveness that made her think she might die. Soon.

Rachel leaps off the bus, urine running down her legs, stinging the scratches of childhood as she runs and runs towards the enormous outstretched arms of her father, a giant of a man, a man who could slay any witch. Except her father is not there. He's not home yet.

Home. A small two-up, two-down cottage, the middle of three built in a row all with whitewashed walls and black window frames and doors. At the end of a short path leading off the easterly gable-end, placed behind a privet hedge, are three adjoining toilets. Rachel enters the middle one. She quickly rips off a piece of newspaper from its string, pulls down her knickers and wraps the paper around the gusset, squeezing it hard until she must let go. It would be very dangerous to have her brothers discover that she had wet herself. For now, she was safe: they would still be at school. But she did wonder how they would make her pay for having the day off, for going on the bus alone, for coming face to face with the local witch.

Suddenly empowered by the thought of what she had survived, Rachel skips around the back, passing quickly by Number Three, where David lives with his mum – but not with his dad.

Rachel is only mildly curious about David: he is too small to play with and, besides, he's a boy, and Rachel has enough problems with her brothers.

She enters through the kitchen door. A warm smell of baking greets her, rising on the thermals from the Cornish range. Shepherd's pie. Saffron buns. A filled kettle gently blows steam from its soot-stained spout.

Sputnik the black and white cat is intently focused on something underneath the Burco boiler. Rachel creeps past, up two stone steps, painted red, through the front room dominated by its new three-piece-suite, and past her father's enormous armchair, set at an angle to fully appreciate the fire, his rolled-up spools of newspaper, arranged like headless flowers in a vase, standing in the brass pot silently waiting to light his cigarette, waiting for the children to fight over whose turn it is to hold the paper in the fire's flame.

And on up the stairs. Tiptoeing. There are only two doors on the landing, the first into her parents' bedroom, where Ruth is asleep, two-year-old Mark, also asleep, nestled in her arms. Mark's soft, chubby cheeks shine like pink tomatoes.

Mum and son are nesting in the warm well created by Jack on an eyrie of a bed with its three mattresses, feather bolster and pillows. Satisfied that all is well in her world Rachel returns to the kitchen, where Sputnik has cornered a mouse.

Her first instinct is to scream for help but she stops herself before she erupts, instead grabbing the cat – really digging her nails in – and somehow gets hold of the small creature, cupping it like a butterfly in her hands, its tiny heart beating explosions against her palms. Sputnik is livid. He claws with his paws up her bare legs.

Rachel prays for the prey as she desperately pushes it out through the letterbox. Then she rests, relieved, as Sputnik stands on his hind legs, bowing his spine so he can reach for the door handle. The mouse runs back in, underneath the door. This time Rachel kicks Sputnik out of the way and forces the mouse back out the way it came. Then she blocks the gap with her body and examines her war wounds. She squeezes the scratches hard until scarlet mushrooms travel like paw prints on sand up her bare white legs. She gives Sputnik a reproachful look; until this moment they had been friends. Sputnik is unimpressed; he's waving his tail, slowly from side to side, growling to be let out.

Rachel leans down and peers underneath the door to make sure that the mouse is clear away.

Sputnik does the same, brushing Rachel's face with his inflated tail. They both watch as next door's tabby spits the dead mouse onto the floor before sashaying out through the garden, tail erect.

Rachel flings the door wide open and shouts out through heated tears: "Get lost!" She picks up the strangely still but hot mouse and can still feel the echo of the heartbeat, feel the pulse of silence. And within this timeless stillness Rachel wonders what it means to be dead.

Rachel isn't sure what happened when she picked up the dead mouse but she feels as though, somehow, the mouse has given her something, and so as a gesture more of gratitude than anything else she steals, from the kitchen, a desert spoon in order to dig a grave. She finds her Sunday School Bible and wipes her face clean for this special duty. Their scrappy garden is small and henpecked, but Harry, who lives at Number One Stamps Lane, has a picturesque cottage-garden, the only garden in the entire area to have Wisteria dripping from its walls, a perfect heaven for a tiny dead mouse that will be buried with all the solemnity that Rachel can muster.

Rachel is small for her eight years; she weighed in at only five and a half pounds. She has her father's blue eyes which, in the winter, can pale to grey. The outer edge of the irises are ringed with a much darker blue and the lashes are black, and long. However, the look that gazes out from these eyes, the disarming innocence which can turn to candid disdain without a blink, unquestionably has slid down through the generations, passed on like a precious genetic recipe, from Granny Opie to Ruth and now to Rachel. And in truth, it is these 'Granny Opie eyes' that render the males of the family, with all their bullish strength, vulnerable. For whether it be a look of contempt or a look of love once caught in their spellbinding gaze, the men are both lost and found.

Rachel slides her spoon beneath the long green leaves of a yellow primrose and digs into the rich brown soil. It is the consistency that flour and lard takes when rubbed together, and when Rachel squeezes it tight in her fist it holds its shape. If she were making pastry, she would add water at this point.

These Silent Skills lie hidden amongst the threads of her mother's apron which, on Rachel, trails to the ground and wraps around her like a sneaky shroud, marking the end of her childhood. Rachel lifts the mouse and is about to lower it into the shallow grave when a sharp stinging slap on the back of her hand sends it flying up into the air.

"What you doing, girl?" Her older brother John (ten) demands while her younger sibling Matthew (seven) picks up her Bible and tosses it to John, who throws it back, and Rachel is at once piggy in the middle, torn between going to find the mouse and saving the Bible.

"Stop it, stop it, stop it!" Rachel is backwards and forwards, trampling the primroses that have become hot coals, branding their destruction onto the soles of her feet, and placing a memory there that she will never quite be free of.

She'd like to cry but because boys don't, neither can she. If she cries she will never belong to their world and will be forced more and more indoors to polish furniture and stand with her hands on her hips, sighing as clouds pass over the sun and the rain means that the washing will not blow freely on the line but pile up in a bucket and hang from string like damp curtains all about the cluttered kitchen.

"I'll tell God!" Rachel screams. "Give me back his book."

"You're weird girl!" Matthew throws the Bible back to John. The boys start their chanting, "Rachel is a weirdo, Rachel is a weirdo."

Rachel stands still, places her hands on her hips, and fixes John with a look of imperial confidence.

"I'll tell Dad." She spins quickly and stares hard at Matthew. "I'll tell dad – and you won't sit down for a week."

The boys, worried, look quickly at each other. Rachel turns, just as John hurls the Bible so that it catches her, not in her back – which was his aim – but directly over her heart. Rachel stumbles backwards, clutching at her chest like an Indian squaw who has just been shot by a cowboy. For a moment, in Harry's pretty garden, all three children become grey statues each stilled by the wondering of whether this is trouble or not?

Matthew is the first to move. He picks up the Bible and rebukes John. "You didn't have to throw it so hard."

"It wasn't me! Rachel moved."

Rachel suddenly leaps up, snatching the Bible from Matthew. "You two are dead when dad gets home." The boys are secretly relieved. Rachel's dry eyes tell them that, despite the threat, she will not be eliciting Jack's help. John is so grateful he immediately seeks out and finds the dead mouse. "Hey Rach, why'd you kill the mouse anyway?"

"I didn't kill it, stupid!"

Very soon and not really understanding the 'how' or the 'why' John and Matthew are chief mourners at the graveside, their heads bowed as Rachel reads from her Bible. "In my father's house there are many mansions . . . " She doesn't know what it means but the idea of a house filled with mansions both intrigues and delights her.

It is, for all three, their first funeral. And later that day, because Rachel 'didn't tell' and Rachel 'didn't die', John leaves on the pillow on her bed a cross, made from two lolly sticks and an elastic band, the word 'mouse' scratched along one length with his school pencil. A sense of honour and humility prevents either of them ever mentioning this small act of sibling love.

Abigail Daylight lives in a galvanised shack set in an orchard enclosed by granite stone walls. Rain dances off its tin roof and smoke leaks from the chimney.

Pear trees cling to the high walls and apple tree boughs bend to the ground. Raspberries and loganberries splash red across green bushes and strawberries hide under green leaves. A small lazy stream passes through lush, rabbit-feed banks and irridescent dragonflies hover in rainbows.

Children's chatter and laughter travels on the wind from beyond and yet, and yet, Abigail Daylight sits in the dim light cast by one oil lamp and a spitting log in the pot-bellied stove, her head bent towards the letters laying in her lap, her heart dried up like a prune.

We used to come to Carbis Bay beach for our Sunday School tea-treats. I was probably about four years old when I first remember it. A coach filled with entire families – children, parents, grand-parents, aunts, uncles, and cousins – and massive hampers of home-baked food. And crates of dandelion and burdock.

We'd driven no more than fifteen miles but we might as well have flown to the Bahamas. We were used to an industrial landscape with disused mine buildings and giant chimney stacks that stood proud above stretches of bramble-covered wasteland. We had small, terraced houses with (mostly) unkempt gardens, where chickens pecked and dogs on chains occasionally stood up to have a bark. Yet here we were suddenly driving through detached, villa-style bungalows with palm trees and Yucca plants in the gardens and glorious displays of flowers everywhere and not one set of onions to be seen. We were somewhere where the road was edged with membresia, growing wild. We were somewhere that seemed so extravagant. That still does.

I clearly remember being awed by it. I would not have known the word 'exotic' but I drank in the exoticism. And although it's changed, and there are now high-rise holiday apartments, too many second-home tourists, and it's known locally to be a place for 'newly weds and nearly deads', I would not live anywhere else.

At 3am the beach is all mine – except occasionally for the night fisherman. All searching for stillness in this chaotic world.

I am trying to remember something, but it's elusive, like a dream. It might be to do with Abigail, but I'm not sure. I do not know why she should be haunting me after all these years . . .

Wishing her dead is not the same as killing her. Finding her dead is not the same as killing her. Even so, she taunts me. And I do not really know if I believe in ghosts. I think it is some sort of displacement.

Rather than think about my father's illness, my mind has given me something else to worry about. I'm very good at displacement.

I do not remember the moment I became afraid of Abigail. I can't even recall a time when I wasn't afraid of her. We were all afraid of her. Weren't we? Us kids, I mean. At least I think the others were afraid. She was like a mythic creature, a female bo-gey man. She was so different and she seemed so ugly.

I know now that she wasn't ugly, just beaten. Did I fear becoming her? It would not have entered my head. I wanted to be like Sarah . . .

Sunday School Prize-Giving

Today is Rachel's day to shine. Even her father is coming and he is strictly a 'funeral and wedding' man. She saves him a seat next to hers, next to the aisle. It is the only free space left and Rachel places her tiny gloved hand on top, thus securing it. It should be a throne bedecked with flowers, but it's a small stacking chair which, at the end of the day, collapses down to fold.

Rachel is dressed in a pale lilac duster-coat and dress, made especially for her by Mrs. Reed her piano teacher. It is the only thing she has which fits perfectly, and within the soft spun cotton, through a process of osmosis, Rachel too is made perfect. She views the rest of the congregation through her new smugness and at once sees their ill-fitting hand-me-downs, their Jumble Sale Sunday-best, and a heavy sense of 'unbelonging' lowers her head with the shame of such unholy thoughts. And like this she remains, aping prayer. And Ruth, sitting next to the aisle, trying to control Mark, who is bored and wriggling in her lap, looks upon her pious daughter, aching to understand why she is always so serious.

In the space that separates mother from daughter sit John and Matthew, contentedly splatting the backs of people's necks with chewed newspaper missiles aimed with precision from their slingshots, each too busy to notice that they are filling a gap. Ruth smiles at her naughty boys and thinks of her husband Jack and hopes he will leave the pub on time. Leave the pub in a straight line. Leave the pub.

Entering, from a side door, into this humble gathering, steps Sarah. Sarah, the Sunday School teacher. Rachel lifts her head and watches intently as the willowy figure with auburn hair steps onto the small stage, bringing with her into this musty gloom the sweet scent of Chanel No. 5. She is dressed in a tightly fitting black suit with a white scooped neck collar and three quarter-length sleeves trimmed with white cuffs. She carries with her, like a clutch bag, a white leather-bound Bible with a zip around it. Sarah sits and crosses her legs, dangling a black patent leather court shoe from her silk-stockinged toe. Rachel, unconsciously, pulls up her off-white socks and eases off one red plastic sandal to dangle from her toe. Who better to aspire to becoming than Sarah?

Joining her on stage, in an aura of self-importance they can't quite manage, is the minister, clothed in a brown, ironed, shiny suit, and, as quickly, his wife, in blue crimplene. Their presence stirs the congregation to stand to sing, and with one rendition of All Things Bright and Beautiful, the prize-giving has no sooner begun. Without Jack.

Who is not too far away.

The Tinners' Arms is owned by Betsy Tremberth but, because she is a widow, many of the village men assume a kind of honorary co-ownership; they may change a barrel, stack crates, chop wood and complete various tasks which fall under the general heading of 'man's work' and Betsy rewards them generously with an extra pint, or bottle of stout to take home to the wife, or a bag of crisps and a bottle of pop for the disconsolate children (sent by their mothers to bring their fathers home) who sit on the cold stone stoop.

Betsy can manage all of these tasks herself. She is a proud, strong woman with an impressive, uphol-stered bosom. But it is in her nature to be gracious to those who wish to please, especially hard-working simple folk who are more honest than they are ingratiating, more thoughtful than they are obsequious. And thus it falls to Jack Tangye to deal with awkward customers.

So while Rachel twists in her Sunday School seat to make better her view of the chapel doors, Jack downs his pint – the last third in one easy swallow – and slips off his rugby club blazer and hands it over to Harry, his neighbour, his work mate and devoted friend.

Harry smiles as he takes the blazer; he knows all too well what is about to happen to the man at the bar who is belligerently insisting that Betsy pour him another pint, although she has told him quietly and firmly that the last orders bell has sounded.

Jack is too tall for the low-beamed ceiling, so he shrugs his neck deep inside his wide shoulders and in two strides is at the bar. Betsy relaxes. Other drinkers drain their pints and throw their cigarettes onto the dark slate floor, grinding them to ash with their shiny Sunday shoes.

In a whirling smog of grey-white smoke the awkward customer turns in response to Jack's question. "Did you not hear the lady?"

Jack has a smoker's voice: slow and lazy as a smoke ring; rich and smooth as chocolate soup; and loud enough to travel the full length of a rugby pitch. But on occasions such as these he lowers his voice to a whisper, compressed through very tight lips. "Did you not hear the lady?"

While the awkward customer strains to listen, Jack's right fist has already clasped the baffled man's collar and, in another moment, with a straight arm lift, his legs are kicking beneath him, like the last quick steps of a hanged man.

After a measured while, Jack turns to Harry. "What do you think mate, shall us let him go?"

Harry is a very small man, indeed he is a model man, a miniature of the real thing, built like a jockey. And he spends his life basking in the light that shines out of Jack. Harry does not know this, would doubt it if he were told it, but he is Jack's conscience. And while this is inconceivable to Harry, Jack depends on him like a miner depends on his Davey Lamp.

Awkward customer has stopped kicking; his face has turned from red, bloated drunk, to pale grey, back to red, and now blue.

Harry takes his time enjoying the deference which Jack bestows upon him and also knowing that, in Jack's mind, Jack is counting: "One – one thousand, two – one thousand, three – one thousand, four . . . "

The current record for a straight arm lift of an awkward drunk is thirty-eight seconds. Harry judges this man to be lighter than the last, and so waits. Waits. And goes on waiting. Waiting for the head of the suspended man to slump forward.

Harry nods.

Jack lets go.

Awkward customer hits the floor.

There is a long loud silence followed by a gasping inhalation and in something approximating empathy, the other customers too breathe deeply.

Jack is triumphant. "Fifty one!" Only Harry understands what this means. He hands back the blazer. Betsy pours two whiskies and the awkward customer crawls towards the door. Jack and Harry chink their glasses and, in unison, knock back the shots.

"Cripes Jack, look at the time! There'll be ructions." Jack looks at the jaundiced ceiling, whistles, and pats his friend firmly on the back. "We're for it – little Rachel's gonna kill me," he says laughing.

"Not to mention what Ruthie will do," responds Harry. They both laugh a little more nervously, wave their goodbyes, and leave in their wake the awe and wonder that a straight arm lift never fails to inspire.

Abigail Daylight wore her lover's coat because she loved him.

Loved him.

Loved him with a passion so deep that after he left her she crawled inside his coat, inhaled his masculine muskiness, felt his silk-lined charm, and got lost in the enormous folds of him. She took with her a bottle of gin and she didn't come out alive.

Leather-Bound Bible

In the small Methodist Chapel, Dora Daniel is the first to collect her prize, followed by her sister Mini, and then her brothers George and Peter. The minister calls their names like a teacher from a register, leaving Sarah to shake the hand of each bemused child before handing them their prize – a small picture Bible given for attendance. The blushing pink children return to their seats, desperately trying to swallow down their smiles.

At last the minister calls, "John Tangye. Matthew Tangye. Rachel Tangye."

Ruth sighs. Jack has let her down. Let his children down. But she pushes the thoughts into the basement of her mind – where she will never find time to deal with them – and does what she always does at times like these: thanks God for the great good fortune to be blessed with a man like Jack who has given her such wonderful children and, with this thought softly illuminating her beautiful face, looks upon her scrubbed children with pride.

John and Matthew race to the front, snatch their Bibles, and return to their seats with as much speed. Rachel has struggled to get her sandal back on and so there is a moment of stillness before she steps forward to walk on the red carpet towards Sarah, who smiles with great affection at her star pupil – and probably the only child who will actually read their Bible.

Rachel has waited months for this moment, has counted the Sundays, and as her small arm reaches towards her prize Rachel suddenly notices that she too, like everyone else, has a small picture Bible, identical to the one she received last year. This shocking realisation recoils her hand, as if she had just fingered fire.

Sarah is immediately concerned, but takes Rachel's hand and presses the small book into it. She continues to hold Rachel's hand and, in a quiet voice, asks, "Whatever is the matter Rachel, do you not like your prize?"

For a moment Rachel hesitates, and then whispers,

"I wanted one with a zip around it." She raises her head and her tear-filled eyes awaken Sarah's maternal heart. But before Sarah has time to respond the minister steps forward. In a loud voice he says, "Return to your chair right now you ungrateful child – or I'll take it back."

Rachel clutches her prize and turns painfully toward the hushed congregation. She is utterly bewildered and can feel inside her the depth of a sorrow so strong it renders her completely alone. And in this palpable 'separateness' she stands bereft, paralysed, unable to return to her seat.

As a small prayer builds inside Rachel the chapel doors burst open, and Jack's massive frame is silhouetted against the light, which streams like a quenching river into 'Rachel's day' which, like her hopes, was turning to dust. Rachel runs along the red carpet into Jack's outstretched arms. John and Matthew quickly follow, as does Mark, despite Ruth's best efforts to restrain him. The Tangye boys pile on top of Jack and Rachel, until they all tumble backwards through the doors.

Sarah walks sedately up the aisle, passing John's and Matthew's Bibles abandoned on their seats, passing Ruth's bowed head, and closes the doors.

The prize-giving continues, if not quite as before. The restless gossips are chewing their tongues. But they will not get the better of Ruth, who raises her head and makes eye contact with the minister, who cannot hold her Granny Opie gaze.

Jack has hoisted Rachel up on top of his shoulders. She is still carrying her Sunday School Bible and is recovered enough to be leafing through its pages, studying the pictures. As long as Jack is close Rachel is happy, made secure by his love, which wraps around her like an invisible velvet cloak.

Harry has Mark up on his shoulders and is jiggling him up and down, and Mark rewards Harry with great bursts of laughter that make Harry feel a warmth inside so vital that tears sting his eyes. Harry has never been married and has no children, so he is deeply grateful for these precious family moments, these moments when pleasure touches pain.

John and Matthew are racing ahead and as they move away from the chapel they can hear the minister's wife strike her piano and the congregation begin to sing "Abide with me..."

Harry clears his throat. "Do you think Ruth will still cook dinner?"

"I'm sure and certain," replies Jack, not at all sure or certain.

This small band of renegades is on their way to the school sports field to play rugby. As they pass the high orchard walls Rachel is able to see Abigail's shack nestled amongst the trees. John and Matthew have scaled the wall and are chanting in unison, "Witch! Witch! You can't get me. Cast your spell and go to Hell!"

"God dammie boys get down and leave Mrs. Daylight be." Jack's stern voice gets their attention, but they do not give in easily.

"Witch! Witch!"

"Will you show some respect for the Sabbath before I show you the back of my hand?" The irony of this request, given their interruption of the prize-giving, is not wasted on Jack or Harry and they are suddenly helpless with laughter. The boys dutifully climb down from the wall, however, and as they do they notice that Rachel is afraid; she has not taken her eyes off Abigail's shack for fear that Abigail might come out, might cast a spell, might do anything. Rachel twists Jack's ear. "Come on daddy, stop being silly."

John and Matthew begin a new and altogether more satisfying chant: "Rachel is a yellow-belly. Rachel is a yellow-belly . . ."

Jack puts on his RP BBC voice. "Will you bunch of reprobates cease and desist."

Rachel who loves to play with words tries to emulate Jack. "Yes cease and desist repro- repro- bates . . . hateful reprobates!"

The boys race ahead, and as Jack and Harry stride purposefully along Rachel can't resist one last look over the orchard wall. From this angle she can see straight in through the small window. Abigail is sitting with her head lowered towards her lap but suddenly looks up through the window and straight at Rachel, with a look that sends a coldness across Rachel's flesh as might a morning fog creeping in from the sea.

Abigail may be looking through the window but there is nothing out there that she is capable of seeing. She turns inward, always inward. Searching for her love. Searching for her life.

Dearest Johnny,

You touched me . . . with your tongue . . . and made me beautiful.

You see? This black ink is already at work saying out loud things that women – Good Women – should not know, let alone utter.

Abigail crumples the letter tightly into her fist. Then a small sublime smile changes the world she sees . . .

It's 1955 and ten years of sorrow has been wiped from her mind.

Abigail walks along the path to the Village Institute, dressed in a pretty floral dress buttoned from the hem to the 'v' of the neck, and a small white cardigan draped over her narrow shoulders. She steps lightly in white heeled shoes and carries a white clutch bag. The sun has blushed her cheeks and her glossy black hair dances on her shoulders. She is thirty years old and as nervous as a teenager.

There's a party inside, organised by Jack Tangye and Harry Thomas and funded by Abigail's father, Arthur Dean, the mine captain.

Betsy Tremberth has set up a makeshift bar. Mrs. Dunstan, who is in charge of the ladies 'bright hour' meetings, has organised a table with tea and fruitcake. A skiffle band tunes up in the corner and a banner written on a threadbare sheet has 'Good luck boys!' written across it in brown paint.

The village is gathered to say goodbye to four tin miners who are emigrating, moving on to Australia.

Abigail's father insisted that Abigail attend. So it is with a certain dread that Abigail leaves her small quiet life and enters the chaos of the Village Institute.

Abigail is naturally shy and feels, despite her outward appearance, clumsy and gauche on social occasions. As she turns the door handle and walks in to the crowd her head is high, but she's acting – only playing out the part her father has written for her. Confident and smiling Abigail walks straight to Mrs. Dunstan and asks for a cup of tea. Seated close by is Ruth Tangye, her proud pregnant belly covered in a dress of blue and white polka dots. Ruth smiles, Abigail smiles back, but too soon has walked away, cursing herself as she goes for missing her chance to say hello. Her head is down now, negotiating the room which is crammed full of strangers, strange people, people. She carries her cup and saucer awkwardly, wishing that she had chosen lemonade and thinking, "Oh God, when will it end? Can it be time to go?" She finds a wooden pillar to lean against, settles herself, takes a sip of tea and at last looks up, straight into the impenetrable brown eyes of Johnny Daylight. Where she is at once caught in the light of his predatory look.

Johnny spotted Abigail from the moment she walked through the door. He followed her. He got the measure of her: a good quiet girl, non-drinker, non-smoker, probably goes to church. Single? Widow? Past her first flush. Still, has nice legs, great arse, and breasts that can be cupped in each hand. Classy. Definitely classy. Kiss her. Tongue her. Inside her, yes . . . yes . . . sweet . . . sweet woman.

Abigail becomes flustered but quickly gathers herself and looks at him with disarming frankness.

He holds out his hand. "Johnny, Johnny Daylight."

In order to shake his hand Abigail must swap hands with her cup, saucer and handbag. Eventually, when she does so, she feels . . . sex. It overwhelms her, courses up her hand, infusing her entire body, moistening tender places that ache with longing. It's quite breathtaking. "I'm hopeless . . . "

"It's very nice to meet you . . . hopeless."

"I mean . . . hopeless . . . at remembering names, and hopeless . . . at do's. These sort of do's. Hopeless . . . at everything . . . Abigail, Abigail Dean. How do you do, Johnny?"

"So all this is down to you." Johnny gestures around the room. He can't believe his luck. The mine captain's daughter! "Is that why you're here – making sure that the workers are content with their crumbs?"

Abigail feels challenged, but not threatened. "My father is paying. Had I a choice, I'd be elsewhere."

"Come on, you need a decent drink." Johnny takes Abigail's cup and saucer and puts them on the nearest table. He grabs her hand and leads her through the crowd towards the bar. His tin miner mates heckle him as he goes. "Setting charges too deep there!"

"Go on Johnny, you'll only get kangaroos where you're going."

They reach the bar. Abigail is worried. She already cares too much. "Is this party for you? Are you one of the men who are emigrating?"

"I'm one of the men who are coming back. Coming back loaded!"

"I don't drink."

"You want to be somewhere else, don't you?"

Rugby And Roast Potatoes

Ruth removes a roasting tin from the oven, holding her head away from the singeing heat. She spoons sizzling fat over the golden chicken which is nesting in the twenty crispy potatoes she peeled before church. Silently, she repeats a familiar mantra: 'That man will be the death of me. That man . . . will be the death of me. That man will be the . . . death . . . of me . . . '

Satisfied and restored she leaves the chicken sitting on top of the stove and goes out in search of her brood. Stepping through hens – now one less – there is a change to her inner voice. "My big strong man with his enormous hands can snap a chicken's neck as if it were a match. John and Matthew fascinated;

35

Rachel screaming from behind her hands, running upstairs . . . refusing to pluck it . . . very often doesn't eat it . . . puny child. Odd child."

Ruth reaches the hedge. Granite stones lie hidden under the verdant grass and weeds. Three stones have been removed, making foot holes. Ruth climbs easily. She's fit and lithe. She has a fluid sensual movement, a graceful physicality. The innocent child still plays inside her. It's almost as if her body didn't know how to grow up – didn't know it had to. She was eleven when her periods started – she'd thought she'd hurt herself running. And it was when John was born, spilling blood over blue and white polka dots, that Ruth discovered a baby came out the same way it went in.

Ruth stands on the hedge watching her family play rugby in their Sunday Best. Jack and Harry have removed their jackets, Rachel her coat, and Ruth would be pleased – if only they were not using these as goal posts.

Rachel has the ball tucked under her arm, holding it tight and close. Matthew and John try to catch her, but Rachel weaves and crouches low enough to reach through Jack's outstretched legs, where he is defending the touch line. Rachel scores. Harry leaps up and down shouting, "Oggie Oggie Oggie!"

From the hedge, Ruth shouts, "Oi! Flipping Oi!"

Then, "I'm feeding the dinner to Sputnik."

The game stops. Jack is resisting telling his boys that they should not have been beaten by a girl because he has other worries. His shirt is covered in mud and Ruth isn't going to forget his late arrival at the chapel.

He turns to Harry. "Fire of life, she'll beat the living day lights out of me."

"No doubt about it."

Jack takes Mark from Harry, using him as a shield as he eyes his wife, trying to figure out how best to play it. He has two options, affection or contrition. He decides on affection – it always works best. Satisfied, he catches up to John and Matthew and cuffs each of them around the head. They turn, both hurt and angry and glare up at him. He answers their unspoken question. "That's for being beat by a runt of a girl."

"You let her through!" pleads John.

"Yeah!" agrees Matthew.

"They have a point," concurs Harry. Jack concedes with begrudging incoherence.

Rachel has been absorbed in her Sunday School Bible, wondering if this new one has a picture of God. The closest she can find is one of Moses. She runs to catch up with Jack. "Daddy, what does God look like?"

Jack looks down at Rachel, sees the picture of Moses and retorts, "Like Moses, only older."

Rachel studies the picture. Moses has a long grey beard down to his waist and grey hair that streams in rivulets over his grey robes. "No one can be older than Moses?"

"Methuselah can."

"Meth- Methy- methesmenna. Stop lying daddy, no one can have a silly name like that!"

Sometimes Jack could laugh and cry all at the same time. His little girl has inadvertently pronounced the Greek word for 'drunk'. (Jack knows this word in several languages, learned during his travels as part of his national service with the RAF.)

"Now you're speaking Greek to me," Jack laughs and laughs. "Would you be accusing your own father of falsifying information?"

Rachel is sensitive enough to know that Jack is laughing at her, but she can't quite figure out why. Nevertheless, she adores these games with him. "Liar! Liar! Teller of tales!"

As Jack climbs the hedge, holding onto a sleeping Mark, Rachel hits him on his backside, hard enough to sting her hand. Jack turns. "I'll be coming after you girl."

Ruth, who has been waiting patiently, slaps Jack hard in the same place. "And I'll be coming after you boy." By this gesture Jack understands that he is forgiven.

I know it's mad – a middle-aged woman talking out loud on the beach. At least there's just you and me, Abigail, and if anyone understands madness it's surely you? Can you hear me Abigail? Don't answer, please don't answer. I didn't mean you any harm. I didn't mean to run away; I was young and frightened. And now I'm older, and just as frightened. I don't know why you've come back. What do you want?

If I can help you, maybe you'll find some peace, and maybe you'll leave me alone, and maybe you'll forgive me, and maybe you'll help my father to live. Just maybe, you are a ghost that can heal?

I hang onto the idea that my father will recover because I do not know how my mother will live if he dies. How will any of us? He must live because he has to. He is the strong one. They are so different – Jack with his drinking and Ruth with her Methodist upbringing. My grandfather used to come back from the pub and had there been women drinking in the bar he would drag my mother from her sleep and beat her with his belt.

"If ever I catch you in a bar, Ruth, you will get more than this. Bring any trouble home to this house and it's the workhouse for you."

Do you remember the workhouse, Abigail? Did

you fear it like everyone else? It's a hospital now. Gran died there. She used to say, "I'd rather die in a broom cupboard than get in a bed in that place." And true to her word, she died in a chair next to her freshly made bed. The nurse had gone to fetch a cup of tea and when she returned Gran was dead.

I don't know why I'm telling you this. Strange isn't it? The person I've feared most is you and not only are you dead but here I am talking to you.

I wonder if Ruth's marriage to Jack was an act of rebellion. If that's the case it cost her dearly, because she hates his drinking. I remember us kids being in charge of spying on Dad with the sole purpose of informing her the minute it looked as though he was sneaking off to the pub. We became adept at recognising the signs: first he'd stand with his back to the fire, then he'd start to jangle the loose change in his pocket, then he'd rock his weight forwards and backwards from his heels to his toes, and then he would be out the door. We always gave him a sporting chance before telling, but one day I remember mum running out of the back door and hurling the rolling pin at him. The distance was about fifty feet and it caught him, square, on the back of his neck, and he was so stunned it nearly felled him. We were all shocked, even mum. But then he smiled and carried on, and I'm sure he was proud. I'm sure after a couple of drinks he would have been bragging about his wife and her rolling-pin-throwing abilities.

Better their tempestuous life than your wretched one . . . I'm sorry Abigail I don't know what you want from me. I can no longer be sure what is true. Some things I remember . . . some things I remember other people telling me . . . some things might exist in my imagination. Some things were in your letters. Is that it, Abigail? You've waited nearly forty years to come and get your letters?

I'm cold, cold to my bones . . .

Dearest Johnny,

Sometimes I think I wanted you more than you wanted me. There was a kind of desperation about my need for you . . . Johnny, it wasn't desperation. It was hunger . . . a ravenous insatiable hunger . . . the same hunger that turned you into a predator and me into . . . into a . . . fool . . .

By the light of the full moon Johnny and Abigail walk slowly up the steep road, a road which will eventually turn into a dusty track that is the foot of

Carn Brea. As music and laughter recede from the Village Institute the silence is taken up with deepening breaths and quickening heartbeats.

Johnny takes Abigail's hand; expectation and potential crackle between their touching lifelines.

Eventually they find a path that winds its way through high ferns and there is something strange, almost mystical, about the very earthiness of this small, rocky promontory that demands reverence. So in silence they continue on their way until they collapse, breathlessly, onto a granite stone boulder known, colloquially, as the Devil's Frying Pan. "More of an egg poacher, aint it?" whispers Johnny, laughing.

Abigail is tipsy. She's never before drank gin, and it's given her a daring she didn't know she had.

Rain has been winning a war of attrition over the granite stone upon which they now lie. Abigail runs her hand over the smooth scooped surface. It is more of an egg poacher. She smiles at him. "How can something as soft as water do this to something as hard as rock?"

Johnny takes off his long black coat and wraps it about her shoulders. "The granite is only pretending to be hard." He lights two cigarettes and gives one to Abigail who shakes her head. "I don't smoke."

"You said you didn't drink, but that didn't stop you . . . "

Abigail giggles. She feels silly doing it, but can't seem to stop herself. "What do you mean the granite is only pretending to be hard? Does that mean that rain is only pretending to be soft?"

"Turns to ice, doesn't it?"

Abigail shivers, and pulls Johnny's coat tight around her. She can smell him, can smell this man on the collar. She inhales deeply. She likes this mix of cigarette smoke, shaving soap, sweat and . . . something else? Something . . . metallic?

Johnny stubs both cigarettes out and places them back in the packet. Then he leans forward and kisses Abigail. He is gentle at first, waiting for her to warm to the idea. Then, once he feels the soft yes of her lips, passionately. His right hand finds the hem of her dress, the silk of her stocking, the satin of her thigh, the heat of her wetness, the slow pulsing grip of her tightness . . .

During three years of marriage not once did Abigail's husband touch her, finger her. There was no foreplay, only penetration, a kind of clumsy, dutiful penile penetration.

Abigail adjusts her position so she can see Johnny's hand between her legs, see his mouth on her nipple, feel his probing finger . . .

Her husband's hands were exquisite. It was the first thing she noticed about him. Long slender fingers, which always held on loosely, that never gripped. He was a kind, compassionate man and despite his quiet, prepossessing nature he had the courage to be a conscientious objector. Abigail admired this in him. Loved him for it.

Johnny's head between her legs now, licking her, licking her. And then, without stopping, he suddenly opens his eyes and looks straight at her. She had no idea people did this. She had never experienced such intimacy, such openness. And he, he, Johnny Daylight, a stranger, with an untold story in his eyes, like the wariness of a captive animal. A prowling animal? Yes, something untamed . . . A wolf. A white wolf.

Her husband was quite asexual. They had been more like brother and sister – having the occasional incestuous relationship – than husband and wife. On the rare occasions they did make love, he entered her too soon, causing pain where pleasure should be . . . It was not like this . . . It was not all-consuming.

Here, on the hard rock, a sleeping volcano erupts, spilling pulsating pleasures . . .

Johnny is at once inside her, hard and explosive. They fit. Fit perfectly. Like a seed within a ripe fruit. When they both come together he doesn't take his eyes from hers, and as aftershocks echo through her body and into the years beyond, Johnny slips out. His energy spent, he takes her hand and guides her finger into her red swollen flesh and makes her taste their hot swcet wanting. Like this they stay, simmering in the shimmering moonlight.

Electric Shock

In the small upstairs bedroom with its sloping ceiling snuggling into the eaves Rachel stands, uneasily, on a small wooden chair. Her little finger reaches up into the empty light bulb socket. A few feet away Mark sleeps peacefully in his cot, which is jammed against the wall by John and Matthew's double bed. Against the other wall is Rachel's single bed, two Bibles and a nightdress hidden underneath her pillow. Matthew is standing on the double bed, mindlessly stepping on Beano comics. He's looking from Rachel to John, unsure what to expect. He's wishing they'd just get it over with. John is standing in the doorway, his hand over the round light switch, finger at the ready. "Right Rachel. One . . . Two . . . Three."

A terrified Rachel nods. John flicks the switch, and then watches in horror as Rachel is catapulted through the air, like a rag-doll tossed from a pram. Her body slams against the wall, slides down it, and lands in a heap on the soft familiarity of her satin quilt. This was beyond John and Matthew's wildest imaginings and so startled are they that they run and hide under the covers of their bed.

Rachel is shaking from head to toe, but she's fine. Her little finger is throbbing and she places it in her mouth. The heat makes the hurt worse, but it does help staunch the tears, which she holds onto with every fibre of her being. She whispers to herself, "I'll be coming after you boys." She hates them, hopes the witch will cast a spell on them and that they'll turn to salt.

John eases out from under the covers.

"Say something Rach. Go on. Please . . . ! It wasn't my fault. You must have put your finger in too far." John sits up, and looks intently at her. "I think she's alive." He pushes at the lump in the bed, which is Matthew. Matthew then crawls out from underneath the covers where he'd been lying in foetal position.

"Please say something Rach," Matthew implores.

"I hate you. I hate both of you."

The boys are both redeemed by this response.

"You should have seen it, Rach. You were flying,"

John says, genuinely proud of his sister and his small part in it.

Matthew stands up, leaps off the bed and throws himself into the wall. "Yeah, it was brilliant Rach."

John does the same and now they are both lying heavily across Rachel's legs.

"Go away! Get lost!" She begins to kick them off. Usually she can't beat them at this – they are too strong and too heavy – but by some intuitive understanding residing within the wisdom of love, John and Matthew allow Rachel to win.

Three Wishes

After school the next day, Rachel, still nursing her wound, a small white scar on the tip of her right little finger – which will stay with her throughout her life – places the same finger into the velveteen thimble of a foxglove. She didn't know that this was digitalis, that it could slow your heart, perhaps even stop it. She learns this later, much later. For now, she just knows that faeries live in such things, and faeries can grant wishes.

With eyes screwed tightly shut, Rachel makes three wishes: "I wish to see God. I wish for a new house. I wish for a baby sister." She opens her eyes and God reveals himself immediately, not as a person but as a luminescent shaft of brilliant white light, a vibrating intelligent energy that descends from the sky and penetrates the ground not six feet from where Rachel stands. Here, in the school sports field, on the touch line, God is an enchanting mix of finely spun strands of silver and gold, dancing a liquid dance of magician's alchemy, flimsy as gossamer, delicate as flakes of snow and yet, somehow, mighty. Caught and made spell bound by this celestial DNA, Rachel's heart soars. "God is light. God is light." But as yet unready for the ways in which this may change her life, she runs home. Runs home in a state of euphoria because, on a level she cannot comprehend, Rachel understands with an absolute certainty that her other wishes will also come true. Of course it might have been a simple sunbeam shining on the solitude of a lonely child's day. Who knows what part innocence plays in the way in which we interpret the world, guided as we are through our senses to arrive at our truth?

Rachel bursts in through the kitchen door. She's hardly able to contain her joy; she isn't big enough for all that she feels.

Ruth is baking pasties, up to her elbows in flour and lard. Glistening cubes of red meat are piled up on a plate, and thinly sliced potatoes and onions spill from the rim of an Earthenware bowl, one of the few surviving wedding presents. Mark is in his highchair, his chubby face and hands sticky with biscuit dough. Ruth is tired and sounds exasperated. "How many more times? Don't crash in through the door!"

"Mum! Mum! I've wished for a baby sister."

"You'll be lucky – I've just sold the pram." Ruth points towards two half crowns placed at the far end of the table, her gold wedding ring covered in goo.

Then John and Matthew stampede down the stairs and through the door, shouting as they go. "Dad is coming! Dad is home!"

Rachel follows them outside. John takes the right-hand garage door and Matthew the left. They open them very quickly as Jack hurtles around the corner in his Ford Anglia, gravel and ash flying up from the tyres as he steps on the brake peddle. The car stops with its nose in the garage entrance. It's not actually a garage, it's a large shed, and although the car fits inside there is not enough room to open the car doors. So Jack gets out of the car, walks around to the rear, lifts the back axle and wheels the car, like a wheelbarrow, into the garage. John and Matthew complete this well-practiced manoeuvre by closing the doors.

Rachel can hardly wait to tell her father the news. "God is light, daddy. God is light." Jack smiles at Rachel and hands her his workbag. "What, lighter than this? Or lighter than these two scallywags?" Jack picks up John and Matthew, one under each arm, and like this they stumble into Ruth's kitchen. Rachel follows, slightly petulant, as her great news is being ignored.

Ruth places a tray of neatly crimped pasties, made shinny with whisked egg and milk, into the oven. Jack drops John and Matthew on the floor and picks Mark up and out of his highchair, lifting him up to the ceiling. And then with one long sweep of his arm, he clears a space and lies Mark down on the table. Jack's large hands deftly loosen Mark's clothing, exposing his plump belly. Jack leans forward and blows enormous raspberries into the soft flesh. A combination of Mark's infectious laughter and the naughty farting sounds has everyone laughing – even Ruth, who should be tired of this by now, but who can't help herself. "That's my boy," says Jack, "nice happy boy, nice soft belly."

Ruth looks at her husband who has managed to make his entrance and snaffle away the two half crowns. She shakes her head slowly from side to side. "Nice soft belly, just like his father's,"

Jack puts his arm around his wife who is suddenly made small by his presence and gives her a big kiss on her cheek, which she then makes a pretence of disliking. "Oh go away and have a shave."

Rachel starts to pull at Jack's shirt to get his attention. "God is light daddy, like the sun."

"So that would be why there are no pictures of God in your Bible. Light is everywhere."

Rachel is awed. She'd heard this at Sunday School

but didn't understand how God could be everywhere but yes, light could.

"Everywhere?"

"Yes," says Jack. "Light is everywhere, even in the blackest black. You ask any of the Tinners, they'll tell you."

Rachel runs up the stairs and into the bedroom where the window looks out onto the sports field. The light has gone but the mystery that is memory shifts it deep inside her and although she can no longer see it she feels it touch her, touch her like the moon touches oceans.

I don't know what to make of that light now, except to say that it did seem real and if I close my eyes I can recall that day as if it still exists in a warp in time . . . Somewhere in all of this I have the sense that I still love God, but Christ knows why . . . And God knows what God is. The insecure, egocentric God of my childhood died in that light. My sister is dead. The new home is now under threat from land subsidence. What can I say about wishes except that they do come true . . . They just don't turn out the way you expect them to.

The Tin Bath (1)

Dearest Johnny,

Are you granite stone or are you water?

Abigail walks along the stony lane clenching her bags with tight, intractable fists, surreptitiously avoiding puddles as she traces steps dissolved in time. There is a tin bath in front of a blazing fire and the smell of 'coal-tar' soap. The water is hot, steam rising up like mist from a pond. Johnny leans his back against one end of the bath, his knees drawn up and emerging like two remote Islands, his white translucent skin testifying to his underground life, to a world of darkness where Abigail can't go. Isn't welcome.

Abigail is angry. She's out of the bath, drying herself. Suspenders next. Then stockings. She looks at Johnny and her blood red heart fills her chest sending a heat, fuelled by the fear of losing him, into her cheeks. "So it's all right for you to be inside me but the moment I try – vainly – to get close to you, you shut like a clam."

Johnny looks up, fixing her with one of his looks. He's never looked more beautiful; youth and innocence at variance with something primal.

"Get close to what, Abbie? This is all there is. No good'll come of you looking for more."

"You don't mean that, that's not true, you are so special . . . "

Johnny stands and steps out of the bath, pearly beads of water racing down his body.

"Come on Abbie, I know how to put a smile on that face." He kneels down in front of her, cupping her hips like a precious porcelain pot in his hands, his tongue searching, quenching . . . Awash with wanton profusion Abigail whispers, "Do you love me Johnny?"

The Tin Bath (2)

John and Matthew have Rachel pinned against the shed door. John is doing the talking for himself and his younger brother.

"Go and ask her girl or else we'll get the witch to curse you."

"No! You ask her!"

The boys push Rachel along the path towards the toilet, eventually giving one big shove so that Rachel bangs into the door. Ruth is inside on her knees throwing up, cursing Jack for being so careless.

"For pity sake go away and let me have some peace."

"Can we play boats in the bath?"

Ruth bolts the door, leaving Rachel unsure if this is

a 'yes' or a 'no', but decides it's probably a 'no'.

"But mu-um . . . Can we mum? Please?"

"Don't but me! Don't fill the bath too full!"

Rachel is already on her way back to John and Matthew when Ruth throws up again. And so within the whitewashed walls of the humble outside toilet a new life makes its presence felt, and worry glows in the sweat on Ruth's brow as she wonders how they'll cope. How will she cope? Morning sickness has never lasted this long before; it was usually over in three months. It's been at least seven this time.

There wasn't a day of sickness with John. He was born at 3am. Nurse Clemo had been so disgusted with him that she threw him to the foot of the bed.

"That's the laziest baby I've ever delivered," she said emphatically. But he was born perfect, not a red mark or a blemish anywhere.

Luke was born, still as a winter moon. He had the smallest white coffin imaginable and the tiniest mound of earth in the cemetery: a molehill planted with daisies.

Rachel was six weeks premature. She was as pathetic as a puppy and pink as the flesh of uncooked rabbit and she never stopped crying. Jack hadn't believed Ruth when she woke him at four thirty in the morning to say, "The baby is coming." He'd been redecorating the bedroom and wallpaper lay in drifts about the skirting boards and small pieces hung from the walls like left-over cheese still hanging in a grater. For a moment he hesitated, wanting to clear up, but Ruth's determined tone had him running up the lane in his pyjamas. And only when he reached the phone box did he realise that he was bare foot.

Nurse Clemo had handed Rachel to him and she fitted into Jack's hand and he was overwhelmed. It was not just her smallness, but how her miniature fists were clenched together, like she was clinging to life. And love stirred inside him, turning him inside out. And in her vulnerability he discovered his own; and buried it.

Matthew uncoiled from inside Ruth like a slimy eel. He had such a long thin body Ruth thought he would never end. Nurse Clemo held his head almost to the ceiling before his feet popped out. And though younger, he now stands three inches taller than John.

Mark almost killed Ruth. She was rushed in a bell-ringing ambulance to hospital for a life-saving blood transfusion and every month since his birth she has suffered the pain of iron injections. She has also systematically refused to have her fallopian tubes tied, making promises all the while that she would be careful . . . Ruth vomits and weeps; it will be five children, a house of seven. How will they manage? Ruth leaves answers to questions like these up to God.

John and Matthew open the coal-shed door and take down the enormous tin bath from where it hangs on a rusting six-inch nail. As they struggle to get it out through the doorway Rachel comes out of the kitchen, her arms full of wooden boats made by Harry. John knocks them out of her hands."You don't need those. Come on, help us."

John and Matthew lift the bath upside down above their heads. Rachel dips down and stands between her two brothers and this six-legged carapace marches down the stony lane through the puddles towards the disused quarry. John barking orders like a regimental sergeant major."Left. Right. Left. Right. Haaaalt."

Rachel loves these games that include her. They reach the quarry. Sharp granite boulders stick up through murky brown water made deeper by autumnal rains. Half of the water's surface sparkles in sunlight; the other half is cast in the cold dark shadow of the far off cliff.

The three adventurers heave the bath into the water. It floats – momentarily surprising and delighting them. They thought it would, but were not certain.

John takes control, making triangles with his arms as he puts his hands on his hips. "I'm Captain and there's an end to it." His mother's stance, his father's words, has the others obeying.

Rachel wants to 'name this ship' but she's afraid that that is for sissies, so she keeps quiet and clambers aboard, crouching down and holding tightly to the rim. The bath rocks uneasily in the water, and then more so, as John goes to the front and Matthew to the rear. "I'm Captain Pugwash," says John.

"I'm Black Beard," laughs Matthew.

As the bath sails from sunshine to shade and out into deeper colder waters, where the brown has a tinge of red, John and Matthew fight about the captaincy.

"It's my turn!" screams Matthew, stepping over Rachel to get to where John stands proud. The bath rolls heavily in the water, and then crashes against a large granite boulder. A jaw-clamping screeching has the children covering their ears. Then John and Matthew lean over the side to inspect for any damage, and the tub tips all three into the gloom. All that had been fast is suddenly slow in the chilling cold. John and Matthew are good, confident swimmers and they quickly scramble to the shore. Coughing and spluttering, and then laughing – with survivor's relief – until they realise that Rachel is not with them.

Rachel has been taken down by the weight of her water-filled Wellingtons. She is mesmerised by the bubbles twirling towards the surface and silly thoughts fill her head. "What would mum say? Worse still, what would dad say? Why go to the quarry when we knew it to be dangerous? Would the mud wash out of these clothes? Where were the others? Lunch would be ready soon: mum sitting in her chair, pulled up close to the range; Sputnik trying to make a dent in her taut boastful belly where her sister was cooking, waiting for her birthday to be born . . . "

John and Matthew stand up and then both enter the water, diving in a short way and then coming straight up for air. They look around them; the mud has made it impossible for them to see though. And panic rises in each of them, like the water in Rachel's lungs. "Go for help! Go for help!" Matthew turns on John's command and runs, runs straight into Abigail Daylight, who has been deaf to their shouts and who remains deaf to beseeching Matthew.

"Please help my sister! Please . . . " As usual, Abigail isn't belonging to any world other than her own . . .

Abigail and Johnny are sitting on the cliff top watching the gulls play on the wind as it whips up from the

sea and travels over the farmland towards Carn Brea.
"Will you write to me?"

Johnny coughs on his cigarette. "Me? Write?"

"Yes. Why not?"

"I've never written a letter in my life."

"Well you can jolly well learn how."

They both look at each other and laugh, and then Johnny teases Abigail, aping her accent.

"Oh I say! I can jolly well learn how."

The wind suddenly drops and for a moment the gulls are silenced. Abigail speaks quietly but firmly, "I will write to you. I will write to you every day . . . "

Matthew pulls at Abigail's sleeves.

"Please come and help us, our sister is drowning." Abigail takes in the scene. It takes her a long time to adjust to this other world, one which normally just orbits around her at an acceptable distance. Matthew pulls her towards the quarry where John is shaking with cold and fear, tears rolling down his cheeks. "Do help," he implores.

Abigail unclenches her fists and puts down her bags and wades into the water. She has an advantage of height and can see Rachel's hair floating like kelp near the surface. She grabs the locks and pulls Rachel's head out of the water.

Rachel is spinning in the light of Jesus who has waded into the water for her, his arms outstretched and his heart wide open. "Suffer the little children to come unto me." He gently hoists Rachel into his arms. "Miracles do happen, Rachel. Wishes do come true."

Abigail lifts Rachel into her arms and somehow manages to lift her precious bags and she walks, dripping, slowly up the lane.

John and Matthew race home, neither daring to turn to look at their lifeless sister.

As the tin bath sinks out of sight the gentle rocking motion of Abigail's walk restores life into Rachel. She begins to inhale enormous gulps of air and starts to cough like an emphysemic miner spitting out the filthy water.

Abigail pays no attention to the small life that she holds in her arms, for she is caught on another current and swept away.

Dearest Johnny,

A sinister realisation creeps across my body like fine cracks over a delicate china doll. I awake at night gasping for air, alarmed by the thought that you don't love me, have never loved me, will never love me . . .

Inside Johnny's cottage, Johnny carries Abigail in his arms up the narrow stairs and into the candle-lit bedroom to the foot of the brass bed . . .

My dear, dear Johnny why have I not heard from you in all these months . . . ?

Abigail shifts the weight of Rachel in her arms and Rachel 'comes to', and is immediately horrified to discover that it is not Jesus who carries her but the local witch.

Ruth is running to meet them, leaving Matthew and John wrapped in towels and huddled by the fire of the open range.

As Abigail places Rachel in Ruth's arms Abigail whispers, "By your love I am made new and also broken." And an understanding harpoons Ruth's bone-weary heart.

Rachel screams, "Please don't let her put a spell on me! Please don't!" This remonstration reassures Ruth that Rachel is going to be all right.

"Thank you, thank you so much, Abigail."

"Mum don't let her! Please don't . . . "

"I am so sorry; it must be the shock . . . " Ruth's words fade in the twilight as Abigail has turned and is walking away. Ruth limply calls after her, "Thank you, thank you so much." And she hugs her daughter close, fiery tears coursing down her cheeks, until anger restores her composure.

"You stupid, stupid child. Wait 'til your father gets home." And then more to herself: "That's the first time I've heard that woman speak in years."

Ruth takes Rachel inside; her daughter has become quite hysterical. "Please don't let her put a spell on me. Promise mum. Please…"

John and Matthew are glad that Rachel is safe but in the instant forgetfulness that is the grace of childhood they cannot miss this opportunity and both start teasing her. "The witch has saved your life Rachel, now you owe her."

"Yeah! You owe her your life girl."

"Your soul belongs to her."

"Stop it the pair of you! Remember that your father will have business with you." Ruth is in no mood for anymore nonsense and, sensing this, the boys move away from the fire. But the seed they have planted in Rachel bores into her, like a hungry worm into wood.

For Christ's sake Abigail, is this what all this is about? Do you think I owe you? You know what? I wish, yes, wish, with all my heart, that you'd let me drown.

Waving And Drowning

Abigail sits up close to the pot-bellied stove. A small puddle makes absorbing patterns on the floor where water has dripped from the hem of Johnny's coat. Her arms are held out, drying the sleeves. She's remembering Redruth Railway Station. The steam train snorting like an impatient racehorse. The guards loading trunks. Parents and loved ones saying tearful farewells to their sons. The only certainty is that the train will pull out of the station and some people will be left behind. Waving. Abigail will be left behind. Drowning.

These men, four in all, go to the other side of the world, so the parting is without the promise of a reunion; it simply floats as a hope about them.

Johnny is in a good, excited mood. He can't wait to

leave, can't wait to get his new life started.

"Best ten quid I've ever spent," he says, seemingly oblivious to Abigail's distress.

This day has been a long dread in Abigail's life and is now all too real.

"You will miss me, won't you? You will come back?" Rachel reaches forward to hug Johnny but he has stepped from the platform onto the train, closing the door behind him. Turning in the window he gazes at her and quickly looks away. Thus this fragmented portrait, forever framed in her mind, becomes the dog-eared photograph she carries in her heart.

As the train travels away, over the parallel tracks, which stretch into infinity but never touch, the love inside Abigail dislocates, leaving her to be with him.

So it begins, here, on Platform One, in the shadow of her life, the slow decomposition of her soul's song.

The Tin Bath (3)

John and Rachel are standing clothed only in towels. They are waiting their turn. Matthew is naked and standing in the Burco boiler, where he hops from foot to foot because the heating element underneath his feet is still hot.

Jack is scrubbing him. "Will you be still? I'll give you something to hop about otherwise."

"But dad it's burning."

"Fire of life! I'll burn you!" He looks to the others. "All of you! Did you not think to take any oars with you?"

John, Matthew and Rachel lower their heads, embarrassed by their stupidity, and then John looks up, his face bright with inspiration. "We don't have any oars!"

"You don't have a boat, but that didn't stop you sailing! You could have used the cricket bats! How is it possible that I have raised such Nincompoops?"

Rachel's shame transforms to a smile.

"Nincompoops! Poopy ninks!" she chuckles.

Then John joins in. "Ninky nonky poops."

And then Matthew. "Poopy nonky nonky ninks."

All three are giggling. And then Jack explodes in a belly laugh. "You children will be the death of me." He can't help really but admire their spirit of adventure and even feels a little proud of it.

Then Ruth enters the jovial scene. "Mark is sleeping!" Everyone is quiet again. Ruth addresses Jack. "So you've given them a good talking to have you?" It's now Jack's turn to hang his head, but not before winking at his children and in a hopeless display of contrition they all four snigger and shake with bottled-up laughter.

Ruth leaves. Alone, in the next room, she laughs. Her daughter survived, as will they all. She holds her swollen stomach, suddenly grateful for the new baby. For what could be more precious than to bring life into this world?

Later that night when the house is hypnotised by slow sleeping breaths Rachel stares at the ceiling, wondering what form the witch's curse will take. John and Matthew must be right. Rachel owes Abigail Daylight her life. Would Abigail sneak up while Rachel sleeps and simply take it?

A fitful sleep follows and the next day Rachel stays close to the house, preferring to help her mum around the kitchen than to be with her brothers.

"I think you should pick some flowers for Abigail," Ruth says absently as she sorts through a pile of baby clothes, looking for things small enough for a newborn. "She did save you, Rachel. You must thank her. Poor soul."

Rachel is taken aback. "No! No! I won't." Rachel runs upstairs and sobs into her pillow, leaving Ruth downstairs, too exhausted to make the climb and too exhausted to argue. She shouts through the ceiling to Rachel. "For goodness sake, go and play with your brothers. Or go and find your father; he's probably next door."

Rachel turns her back to the world and, facing the wall, finds sleep.

The Tin Bath (4)

Harry is standing on the edge of the quarry. He's holding a bundle of clothes and looking anxiously into the water.

Something dark stirs near the surface, and then suddenly breaks through, Jack emerging completely naked, the tin bath upturned over his head. Harry laughs. "Well done Jack, Ruthie'll be pleased about that. But how you gave her those children I'll never know."

Jack looks at his friend. "It's flaming freezing in there; but you look like you could do with a swim."

"I'd rather have a drink."

Jack snatches his clothes. "Good plan my friend. A jolly good plan."

If I lose my father I will lose all that I am. For somehow it is he who defines me. And I am afraid that without him there will be an ensuing madness that will bind me to Abigail as if to my twin. I am not so disillusioned as to think, for one moment, that I existed for her. I did not, not really. Her job in my life was to pull me from the quarry; she did that. My job in her life was to find her corpse; I did that. So why is she here? Why can't I get her out of my head?

The Down Line

Abigail sits alone on a bench clutching her bags. She's on Platform Two of Redruth Railway Station. It's the down line. From here, eight years before – the year that Rachel was born – Johnny Daylight's coffin was unloaded from the train . . .

Abigail is remembering; her mind knows of no other way in which to think. She cannot engage with the present nor with the future; for her, living in the past is both habitual and a destructive act of will.

Abigail stands stoically beside her father. He is here at her behest; it's the only thing she's asked of him in the last two years. Two years where, taken by an unhealthy love, she has spent her time in a spiritual desert. Indeed she is still there, drinking from the sand that renders her thin.

A large group of mourners accompanies the body to Carn Brea village chapel where the funeral service is held. Johnny was the victim of a mining accident. Solidarity brings these men and women together to praise God – that there by his grace they are alive. The vicar tells of Johnny's bravery, of how he had been orphaned and evacuated from London to the village during the war, and such was his contentment that he returned later to become a miner. Not much is known about the accident. Not much is known about him.

But Abigail, who sits quietly near the back, did know him – saw things in him that no one else could see. She could feel his sorrow hiding in every sinuous muscle. Could feel his fear masked by his strength. Feel his silent dry tears when they made love and his life coursed out of him and flooded into her.

When the procession reaches the cemetery Abigail stands back at the committal service. It is a brilliant winter day: the sun weak and low in the sky; the granite stones of Carn Brea made prominent by the hibernating vegetation.

A strange calm descends over Abigail; Johnny did after all come back to her. At last she knows where he is, and one day she will join him where he waits for her. She turns away, the burial as yet unfinished, and walks towards the Village Institute. The place of their first meeting is now prepared for his funeral tea.

The village women drop into a reverential hush as Abigail glides through them. She's like a ghost, caught in the hinterland between the living and the dead. However, there is a compelling stillness about her as she makes her way to the back room where inside she finds Johnny's storage trunk, packed with all the things he didn't think he'd be able to make use of in Australia. She opens it and, on top of a pile of neatly folded clothes, rests his winter coat and his winter shoes.

Abigail removes her shoes and slips her feet into Johnny's. They're only a little too big and she gathers the laces tightly and ties them in a double knot. Then her arms run through the silk lining of his sleeves as his overcoat envelops her, bringing her a warmth which she buttons to her neck.

She leaves the room, passing once more through the women and their husbands who have now joined them and who, one by one, fall silent as she passes from this world into the still bright day.

Dearest Johnny,

My dearest Johnny Daylight, all I have left is your name . . .

Letters

John, Matthew and Rachel have tiptoed into their parents' bedroom; they are inspecting the new furniture. The old tall boy has been replaced with a chest of drawers; it stands in front of the window, its gleaming veneer reflecting the sun. The children are fascinated by how easy it is to open the drawers, and thrilled when they discover it's possible to do so with just a little finger. Then Rachel accidentally pushes at the top and it lifts up, revealing a vanity mirror and a small compartment filled with papers. Sticking out amongst birth, marriage and death certificates are a small bundle of letters tied with a lilac ribbon. John snatches them up. "What are they?"

"Letters stupid!" retorts Rachel.

"Let me see." Matthew tries to grab the bundle but

Rachel beats him to it and carefully unties the ribbon. "It's joined-up writing. You read them out to us John."

"I've got a better idea." John takes the letters and runs from the bedroom, hotly pursued by the other two. The time then passes with the children happily 'playing postmen', pushing Jack's love letters, written to Ruth when he was stationed in Germany, through letterboxes in the village. As is the way of small communities, these cherished letters are received, opened, read, swapped, blushed over, gossiped about, denigrated and, above all, envied. It will be quite some while before they are returned and burned.

Their task complete, the children decide to have a proper race home. The boys have given Rachel a head start, so while she runs ahead they count to fifty. For some reason Rachel always laughs when she runs, and this makes her weak. She wants to take these things seriously, like her brothers, but no matter how much concentrated effort she applies, her imagination always takes her elsewhere. "Come on boys! Where's your killer instinct! You want to be men, don't you?" This is what Jack shouts at his sons as they hurtle towards the touch line, trying to please their father, trying to make him proud. Alas these words don't inspire Rachel, and she turns to see if her brothers are off the starting blocks and as she does she bangs straight into Abigail, knocking her to the ground and smashing her bottle of gin in green glassy shards across the road. Abigail's glasses have fallen off and, for a moment, she is completely stunned. The boys catch up: John first, Matthew a close second. "Oh my God! Rachel, you've killed the witch! Now you're for it."

This is too much for Rachel and she bursts into tears. "Shut up! She's not dead." Rachel is not too sure though. What would it mean if she were dead? Would Rachel be free or sent to hell?

"She's dead drunk you stupid girl!" John remembers the race and runs off. "I'm going to win."

Matthew follows, right behind him, his long lean legs making easy work of keeping pace with his older brother.

Rachel is left behind, helpless, and then the 'dead' witch moves and Rachel, far too terrified to offer a helping hand, discovers the fuel of adrenaline and runs. She doesn't stop to look back. Yet something of this moment follows her, clinging to her heart as it thumps at her ribs. It feels sinister, like a crow flying over her future, and she knows that one day there will be a reckoning.

They cross the finishing line – the kitchen door. John's first, Matthew second and Rachel third. They find the table laid as if for a birthday party: cold pas-ties, sausage rolls, sandwiches, crisps, cakes, jam tarts, clotted cream, bottles of cola and dandelion and burdock.

Ruth is dressed in a pretty, yet faded, polka dot ma-ternity frock and Jack and Harry are already changed out of their overalls. Mark sits in Jack's arms, pulling at Jack's ear. The breathless children are speechless and look from each adult to the table and finally to Jack for explanation.

"It's a fine thing when a working man has no help to park his car. Especially when that working man has news of gargantuan proportions."

"What is it daddy? What is gar- gar- gargantuan proportions?" Rachel asks, grateful to be rescued from her terrifying visions of Abigail Daylight lying in the gutter.

"We are relocating. We are moving to a new abode!"

From the shoreline I walk back towards the cliffs. There is enough moonlight to locate the footpath and at the bottom I find a rock to sit upon while I lace up my boots.

Yesterday's rain cascades in small streams through the long ferns and over the moss-covered stones until it falls, in moonlit pearls, onto the beach through the roof of a tiny cave. It's enchanting, like a fairy grotto, and, for a moment, I indulge in a fantasy where elemental folk with dragonfly wings wave their magic wands and all becomes well in the world. Then I remember that wishes do come true; at least that is if you are innocent enough. So for me wishes can only ever be ephemeral hopes, forever drowning in the shallows of my consciousness.

Granny Opie did not believe in magic. She thought that we were all possessed of special intuitive powers but that these were actually quite ordinary; most of us were just too lazy to ever make use of them. She used to say, "Some people could cross a railway track and not see a steam train coming straight for them." She reckoned that she knew – knew with an absolute certainty – that Granddad was dying long before the doctor took any notice. "I lost him slowly by degrees."

She was standing in the kitchen of her granite stone cottage and I was restless to be going back home, but something in her manner stilled me. "You shouldn't look at the world through your eyes. You must look with an open heart." Then she fixed me with an all-knowing look and began to weep and, seeing her weep, I wept too.

Granddad choked on the blood-speckled porridge that filled his lungs until he drowned. This was the legacy of his tin-mining life. I have only one enduring memory of him and that was of an old man lying in bed right next to an open window. He was propped up on pillows and wearing blue and white striped pyjamas. He was leaning towards the breeze as it wafted the flimsy curtains, his rasping breaths sounding like Sputnik's purrs, and I took it to mean he was happy. I never saw him again. But I think of that day and Granny Opie and I wonder if she wept because she knew that she too was dying and she was already saying her goodbyes. Granny Opie died within a year of her husband and, reflecting on her, I come to realise the poignancy of a word as simple and as common as 'goodbye'.

We children did not attend her funeral. We were left to wander through the wake, soaking up platitudes and scoffing Auntie Doris' home-made puddings. Aunt Doris loved to create gingerbread men, éclairs, Eccles cakes and saffron buns. We could not wait to see her. We could not eat them all. She wore a flour-dusted apron all the time. I can see the floral pattern stretched around her enormous middle as she cracked eggs and sifted sugar icing. Hers was the only house to be greedy in. She was tear-stained laughter and Sunday tea. She was fresh loganberries and clotted cream. She was very fat. Aunt Doris baked cakes for us but really for her two children who burned in a fire. They died on her birthday and tears glazed her cherry cheeks like the icing on her buns.

I begin the climb up from the beach. Here I feel safe and secure, remembering when scores of children ran naked in and out of the sea. Where they laughed as they buried their fathers in the sand. Where their watchful mothers gossiped as they handed out tea-treat buns the size of side plates to eager sandy hands. All of us ignorant of sun-induced skin cancer, all of us covered in chamomile lotion at the end of the day and itching to shed our pink skins.

I am afraid to open my heart and see all there is to see. There is this half-remembered dream that slips in and out of my mind like a nagging doubt. I have an ominous feeling that Abigail is here to show me something. Something bad. And although I have no evidence – besides a feeling of impending doom – I am convinced that my father is leaving soon. Here in this happy place I believe Granny Opie; I believe my intuition. And I am made miserable by it.

I reach the top of the cliff, numb now with cold, and I sit on a wooden bench and will not budge until I see a shooting star.

The day Rebecca was born was the day I felt all things in life were possible. I don't think I've felt that way since . . .

Rebecca, Beccy, Bex

Jack is sitting at the bottom of the stairs, taking up three steps. He's smoking, well into his second pack. John and Matthew are three steps up from their father. They have polished horse chestnuts suspended on string and are playing conkers.

Rachel is on the top step, her hands in the prayer position. She's praying with such intensity that her palms stick together with sweat.

"Please God let it be a baby girl. Please God let it be a baby girl. I promise to look after her . . . "

Every now and then the boys chant, "We want a boy. We want a boy."

Mark is blissfully unaware, lying asleep in his cot.

Jack draws deeply on his cigarette. It is ominously quiet . . .

He carried Luke in such a tiny white coffin. It broke his heart when he lifted it – the unbearable lightness of it. Leaving the cemetery he could hardly walk, such was the lead that cloaked him. Ruth's eyes! Filled with so much sorrow and no reproach they went straight to his core and his dear children, not really understanding but gingerly stepping through their parents' grief in reverent whispers.

Oh! How did she survive Mark? Blood splashed everywhere, running down her milky thighs, and all she wanted was to hold their baby and gaze at his wonderful little face. She appeared so diminished, lying, lost, in the hospital bed, as vulnerable as their newborn. He didn't deserve her . . .

An in-breath becomes two, as if these thoughts require more oxygen.

A sound of a wet hand slapping, followed by a louder silence, concentrates his mind. Another slap. A short plaintive cry. More silence.

The door opens and Nurse Clemo steps over the children and marches down the stairs, her face red with anger and the effort. Jack leaps up. Now the moment has arrived the time seems to have passed too quickly; he is not yet prepared for what she has to tell him.

"I told you last time to leave that poor woman alone! You have a daughter! A perfect little girl and God knows why but Ruth is fine! I had to slap that baby twice to make her cry, yet she delivered with her eyes open. I've never seen anything like it. She'll be an angel that one, you mark my words."

Jack picks Nurse Clemo up, squeezes her tight and then drops her. She calls after him, "Let this one be the last or I'll chop it off!"

Jack is climbing the stairs two at a time, fighting back his tears. The boys, not in the least bit interested in a new sister, shuffle off; they have eminently more important things to do.

Rachel is thanking God. She stands at the threshold while Jack kisses Ruth, who is flushed with mother-love.

Ruth holds the baby like the pictures of Mary holding Jesus, and for a moment Rachel is not sure if she is allowed to enter such a hallowed scene.

"Come on then, you got your wish." Ruth smiles at her first daughter.

Rachel slowly enters the room and when first she sees the baby she gasps with wonder. It is the most beautiful thing she has ever seen. Now her life will be forever changed. She reaches out and tenderly touches her little sister.

"What shall we call her?" asks Ruth, captivated by Rachel's enchantment.

"Rebecca," Rachel responds without hesitation, as if she had thought of this long ago.

"Little Beccy. That's lovely," says Jack, and here they all agree. And while Rachel gazes into the tiniest of the Granny Opie eyes Jack reaches into his pocket and pulls out all the love letters that have been returned to the house during Ruth's confinement. "These are yours I believe."

"How come you have them?"

"Your delinquent children posted them to the neighbours."

"Oh God Jack tell me they didn't."

"'fraid so. Even Mrs. Dunstan had one."

"Oh dear God! How will I ever sit in that chapel again?"

"On a cushion?"

Ruth and Jack laugh hysterically, melting the tension that had gathered in their bellies like winter snows. The worst had not happened. All was well. And it is not without a little smug satisfaction that Ruth rests her head back into the pillows, imagining the Bright Hour ladies shocked by Jack's passion.

Sensing she may be questioned about the letters Rachel makes her escape, although nothing could dim her joy today. Not even Abigail Daylight. Rachel quickly wipes Abigail from her mind. No! Not even Abigail Daylight. And as subtle as twilight Rachel's skipping turns into a walk and an observant eye might notice a gentle sloping of her young, narrow shoulders.

Rusting Barbed Wire (1)

Abigail grips the rusting barbed wire, which encircles the yawning mouth of a disused mineshaft. She's staring into the gullet of her world, feeling the stagnant warm breath of cheap lives, listening to the echo of crippled backs, lung disease and accidental death, and wishing that she could be swallowed whole. If she were to lean heavily against this wire it might snap, and then she would at last join Johnny. It wouldn't take much strength but it requires a deal of will . . .

This waiting has me defeated Johnny. I have nothing left. I feel more and more that I was possessed of a madness that both mimicked and mocked love. Tell me I'm wrong.

I am lying in the sump of a mineshaft and . . . and . . . I am . . . I am a wretched sight.

The Cattle Truck

The Tangyes' brief, hand-me-down history is precariously piled up on straw in the back of a cattle truck. Incongruously, on Ruth's insistence, the bought-on-higher-purchase furniture sits in the lane to be loaded last, to be covered up with the bed linen already on-board. Much to Ruth's chagrin the chickens will be travelling along with their worldly possessions, but she is too tired right now to argue.

Finally, the slatted gates close, the door rolls down and Harry and the farmer drive up the lane – passing the hands-on-hips women who have come out to bring warm apple pies and wave them on their way.

Jack, Ruth, John, Matthew, Mark, Rachel, Rebecca and Sputnik are crammed into the Ford Anglia.

Everyone is excited and happy except for Ruth. She

is leaving the place where she has borne her children and her mind will not let it rest, will not accept . . . (What could she hope to do to make the new place home? How did Jack, out of all of the possible candidates, persuade Arthur Dean to let the bungalow at a rent they could afford? Arthur Dean! Not known for his generosity, he lets Abigail wander the streets like a tramp, his own flesh and blood . . .)

Jack squeezes his wife's thigh. "You'll be alright, missus. Don't go worrying."

With that, Ruth bursts into tears, and Jack fixes his attention on the number plate of the truck as they pull up at the junction. He grips the steering wheel tight and allows himself one last look in his rear-view mirror . . . (Of course the pub will be further away and Harry won't be next door anymore, but they'll have so much more room in this house and it'll only be a short walk to work; he'll even be able to go home for his dinner. Then there's the massive garden – plenty of land for growing potatoes and onions. Perhaps he could even fix up the greenhouse for tomatoes? It'll be grand. Ruthie will soon get used to it.)

Sitting on the back seat, squeezed up against the window, Rachel holds on tightly to her baby sister . . . (Is it possible to be happier? All of my wishes have come true. Now I will never have to walk past the orchard ever again. I will never be afraid ever again because I will never see Abigail ever again. My brothers will have no reason to tease me. The witch will vanish. And I will always have little Becky and little Becky will always have me . . .)

Then, as if by some unholy sorcery, Abigail is standing beside Rachel, only a thin sheet of glass between them. And she is looking deeply into Rachel's horrified eyes, fixing her with a strange look of knowing, as if, suddenly possessed of clairvoyant powers, she had seen the girl's future, and was perhaps wishing she had let her go down in the water, had let her drown. Rachel cannot bare such scrutiny and tightens her grip around Rebecca and says, too loudly, "I wish you were dead!"

This simple thought, given voice, stamps the moment with a palpable force that seems, suddenly, to live independently in a parallel world where its echo patiently builds momentum.

"Rachel! Apologise! At once! We're all sad to be leaving but there's no need to take it out on that poor wretch." Ruth turns as Jack pulls away from Abigail, too late to say sorry, sorry for her children's jeers, sorry for her ungrateful daughter, sorry for Abigail's poor broken heart, sorry for not trying harder to be a friend . . .

Abigail!

You have got to be kidding. There is no way on this earth that I caused your death simply by wishing for it! Enough of this madness. Fuck off. Fuck the fuck off.

Fade To Grey (1)

Abigail stands still, appearing, like all the other neighbours, to watch the departure of the Tangyes. Rachel turns and looks as Abigail's form slowly transforms into a silhouette, and then vanishes.

Abigail is having one of her better days, one of her better rememberings . . .

I miss your body Johnny, its neat and compact shape. And I miss, when naked, your vulnerability; how I could, simultaneously, see all of your power and all of your weakness and how somehow these things cancelled each other out, so that what I was seeing became more real, more essentially you. I could not get enough of you. I could not give you enough. I was made shameless . . . and open . . . you penetrate . . . physically . . . we pulsate. I remember.

I will always remember . . .

Abigail turns to find her way home.

Proper Job Bath

The drive to the bungalow is a little under a mile and yet the terrain is dramatically different. As they near their new home they find themselves lost amongst tin mines and gravel pits, disused mine shafts, South Crofty's working head gear, ferns fields and small rivers that run red. Steam blows out of the earth and albino-skinned men with Cyclops' eyes surface for air.

"That's where your dad works hard for his living." Jack points to the fitting shop, and the children's heads turn in all directions, fascinated by their new world.

"You've heard of Dolcoath Mine?"

The children nod eagerly.

"Williams Shaft plunged three thousand eight hundred and fifty feet deep into the earth! It was the queen of mines – although," Jack adds, with a wry smile, "not nearly as deep as your mother can be."

Jack glances at Ruth, hoping to see a smile, but she is turned to stone. He slams hard on the brakes and orders everyone out of the car. They all obey except Ruth, who sighs and stays put with Sputnik, now curled up in a tight ball on the parcel shelf below the rear window.

"Now look at this." Jack strides towards a hedge which looks like a boundary to an ordinary field. He takes Becky from Rachel, holding her in one hand and, with Mark in his other, peers over the hedge.

"Now children, be careful. I want you to climb up just so that you can see over the top. Do be careful now."

John, Matthew and Rachel do as they're told, and once they look over the top they all exclaim, "Water! A field full of water!"

"Now I don't want any of your messing with tin baths or any other marine vessels on this water. Do you hear me?" The children nod.

"This is far too dangerous and I have spies all around here and I will be the first to know. Have I made myself clear?"

The children nod, still staring at the huge expanse

of water with tiny ripples blowing across it.

"But dad, why is the field full of water?" John is not so stupid that he thinks water is growing in the field but he, like the others, is very perplexed. There is something sinister about it, not just the potential danger of drowning, but to do with the world not being quite what it was normally. A field full of water! It made no sense. The children shiver.

"Come on, back in the car." They return to Ruth who takes Rebecca in her arms and Jack drives on.

"Those pumps Harry and I make pump water out of the mine; if ever that field's empty the miners will drown."

"Miners drown anyway." Ruth thinks of her father's lungs filling up.

"I'm gonna be a Tinner!" shouts John.

"Me too," concurs Matthew.

"Over my dead body." Ruth is emphatic, and everyone knows that the subject is closed.

Very soon they are all distracted by Harry waving at them as they arrive outside the bungalow. The garage, complete with mechanic's pit and pointed slate-tiled roof is bigger than the cottage they've just left, and only Ruth takes the time to notice that Jack will never again need help to park his car.

Like Ruth, the children are quiet now, wary visitors in a foreign land. They get out slowly from the car and walk through its imposing gates where they gawp at the bungalow which, until now, had been obscured by long established oak trees. It is a massive four-bedroom, granite stone building, rendered in places with pebble-dash. Other walls are whitewashed, and the timber window frames are painted sky-blue to match the garage doors and garden gates. On the front is a large conservatory that sticks out into an overgrown garden where the grass is at least eighteen inches high. There are two fig trees and a fishpond in the bottom left-hand corner, and a tumbled down greenhouse in the right. The children notice that every tree is ripe for climbing.

A gravel path surrounds their new home like a moat and scrunching noisily they all follow Jack around to the back door where, through a dark hallway, they find themselves in the biggest kitchen they have ever seen. They stand in its centre, nobody quite wanting to fill the space with noise.

"Well missus what do you think of this then?" Jack looks to Ruth, who remains speechless, and then to Harry.

"I think you should fire up that Aga, Jack, and we can get some tea." Harry with his simple request has broken the silence and the children begin to swarm all over the house where their high-pitched voices reverberate off the walls.

"Look! Look!" shouts John. "Matthew! Rachel! Come and see . . . "

John is standing in the bathroom. In the middle is a roll-top-tub standing on clawed feet. He turns the taps on and water shoots out in congested spurts. Matthew, Mark and Rachel enter the room just as John flushes the toilet. "It's all indoors!" he exclaims brightly.

"It's a mansion!" Rachel says. "In my father's house there are many mansions! I wished for a new house and got a mansion. It's the light don't you see?" She leans over the tub and puts the plug in place.

"You're so weird – go play with your new dolly," John says as he watches, amazed, at how quickly the tub fills. Then all the children, by some silent osmotic gesture, smile at each other and begin to strip off down to their underwear. Very soon they are taking it in turns to dive in at one end and re-surface at the taps, waves of water spilling onto the linoleum floor.

Jack and Harry have a four-foot-high gas cylinder which they have procured from the mine. They light the torch and, with flames almost licking the ceiling, pass it through the cinder drawer of the Aga. It is not long before the heart of the house is beating for them.

Meanwhile, Ruth has rescued Sputnik from the

car, fed and changed Rebecca and placed her in her pram. Ruth sits on a tea chest in the middle of her new front room, where all of the furniture from their small life fits into this one room and still leaves an empty space. The worry of how they will ever afford to stay in such a large place claws at her stomach lining like a dog at a closed front door. She finds her apron, a box of food and, with sleeves rolled up, walks resolutely towards her new kitchen, within her new home.

That evening, sitting around the kitchen table, familial love weaves its spell and Ruth leans back in her chair casting her eyes over the plates wiped clean with chunks of home-baked bread. The knives and forks placed so and she touches her angry belly, assured that her ulcer has gone back to sleep.

"Well, what do you think children – shall we give Harry an apple?" Jack asks, and the children – recognising his mischievous twinkle – shout, "Yes!"

Ruth giggles and takes from a wooden box in her pantry – a room of which she is suddenly proud – an apple wrapped carefully in sheets of old newspaper.

"Give it to Harry then. Let him see it." Jack in Master Magician mode.

Harry takes the apple, turns it around in his small hands, holds it to his nose, and smells it. "You scrumped this from Abigail."

The mere mention of Abigail has Rachel running to the pram where Becky lies safely asleep.

"Did I say that you could get down from the table young lady?" barks Jack, but playfully, smiling at his daughter, now frozen in her tracks. Rachel returns to her seat, reassured that Becky is safe – for now anyway. She is worried, worried sick; she should not have wished Abigail dead. She certainly should not have wished her dead while holding on to Becky.

Jack takes the apple from Harry and braces his left fist firmly against the table top, his thumb sticking up towards the ceiling. In his right hand he holds the apple high in the air and then, glancing around the room to ensure rapt attention, quickly smashes the apple down over his thumb, where, to everyone's delight and Harry's amazement, the core pops out.

"Bet you've never seen that before?" Jack laughs at his astonished friend. Harry cannot help but laugh himself in response. And very soon laughter is filling the whole home, spreading from one to the other and from room to room like wild fire, promising the Tangyes a bright new future.

It is only Rachel who notices the small worm wriggling about in the apple core.

Who Else's Vomit Would It Be?

The long summer holidays stretch out before John and Matthew who, at last, can begin building their tree house. Clambering up the sturdy branches they barely notice Rachel pushing, Becky through the garden gates in her pushchair; or Ruth chasing after them with Becky's bottle. "You've forgotten this, Rachel! Give her the banana. And don't let her eat too fast – she'll choke. And don't talk to strangers. And I want you back in two hours. Okay? Answer me, Rachel!"

"Yes okay!" Rachel places the bottle in the duffle bag, which is hanging from the back of the chair. Ruth tries to kiss Rachel goodbye but Rachel turns her head.

"You're never too old for a kiss you know," Ruth rebukes, dismayed by the speed with which her children are growing up. Rachel shrugs and sets off down the lane towards the cemetery.

Rachel has become fascinated with the overgrown tombstones, even beginning the task of clearing them of the thick ivy and tenacious brambles, which she hacks and saws through with a potato knife (stolen from the kitchen). After an hour's labour, and coinciding nicely with when Rebecca wakes, they sit together on a gingham tablecloth and enjoy a picnic together before returning home. Four happy days have passed in this way and Rachel is beginning to see some reward for her hard work: the tilted granite tombstones covered in lichen are clearly visible now, and it is possible once again to make out the inscriptions.

She has never felt afraid in the graveyard. "It's not the dead you have to fear but the living," Granny Opie used to tell her as they tended Granddad's grave. Yet today, as Rachel pushes through the heavy wrought iron gates, she is filled with a sense of foreboding. A light summer wind, chilled by the shade of the tall trees, whips around her bare arms, and she reaches for her jumper, suddenly grateful that Ruth insisted that she take it with her "just in case". She glances at Becky to see if she too is cold, but Becky is fast asleep, her head lolled to the left, saliva staining her pink bib. The crows in their high nests are screeching loudly and where this has never before bothered Rachel it is suddenly menacing. She thinks to turn around to leave immediately, but this seems silly – she's so close to finishing what she's started. So, despite her intuition, she carries on, very soon absorbed again in her work.

Rebecca wakes suddenly and Rachel lays out the picnic things, mashing a banana in a plastic bowl and feeding it to Becky while she sits up, as far as she can. "You are a good baby," Rachel coos, her earlier fears quite forgotten. But then a chill wind passes through her and she turns to find a crumpled sheet of Basildon Bond blowing down onto the chequered picnic cloth. Then another. And another.

Her first reaction is one of long-suffering frustration; she has spent almost a week cleaning up the cemetery only to have people spoil it with litter. So she huffs and puffs, as Ruth would do, picking up the tumbleweed paper balls and stuffing them into the duffle bag. Then, overwhelmed by a deep curiosity, she leaves Becky and follows the paper trail, no longer attempting to clear it up but inexplicably compelled to discover where it is that it's coming from. Then she stops. Alarm coursing through her being. Rachel recognises Abigail's abandoned bags strewn across the narrow pathway, crumpled letters spewing from them. Rachel turns quickly in all directions, searching for Abigail, knowing her to be close.

She hasn't thought about her for months. If she had, it would only have been to think that she was at last free of her. Where was she? She steps backwards, afraid of everything that Abigail will do to her. Then she falls over Abigail's outstretched legs. She quickly stands up, and despite all the good sense that tells her to leave, she looks first to Abigail's worn shoes, slightly too big with frayed laces tied in a double knot, and then the hem of her grubby coat, and then her bony jaundiced fingers gripped around her neck, and then her face, dark as an ink blue sky, yellow bile seeping from the corner of her mouth where flies were drinking up her wretchedness, and finally her blood-red eyes, protruding from her head.

Rachel reels backwards, falling, stumbling, clumsily crashing over the mounds of earth filled with decomposing bodies, hurtling through banks of stinging nettles and tangled shrubs, racing around tombs, until, at last, she finds the gates and like 'this little piggy' that Becky likes so much 'she ran and she ran all the way home'. Pursued by the strange echo of her past . . .

"…I wish you were dead. Rachel's killed the witch.

Now you owe her. She has your soul girl. Wishes do come true. Miracles do happen…"

Rachel runs straight into her mother's arms and pushes herself against her, but no words can come through her breathless sobs.

"Rachel, whatever is it? Where's Rebecca?"

"Where did they go?" Jack asks, already going through the door.

Ruth shouts, "To the cemetery." And then screams at the boys. "Don't just sit there! Go after your father!" John and Matthew leap into action. "Not you Mark. Rachel, calm down, you have to tell me what happened. Is Rebecca safe? Have you been hurt? Has someone touched you? Please Rachel, talk to me. Tell me, is Rebecca safe?"

All Rachel can think is that she has left little Rebecca alone with the dead witch, alone in a cemetery half a mile from home. For this she will surely go to hell. She closes her eyes and tries to get rid of the images of Abigail's contorted face and at last whispers, "I have killed the witch. I wished her dead. I wished her dead."

Jack is running for his daughter's life towards the cemetery, not daring to wonder what may have happened. What he'll do if anyone has so much as breathed the same air as his girls.

In less than eight minutes he is through the gates, and in another two he has swept Rebecca into his arms, still strapped into her pushchair. He has a moment of sheer relief that almost makes him weep, before his sons catch up. "What kept you?" he asks, beating back the softness of his heart. "Pick up these things." The boys do as they're told, sharing the bag of crisps that Rachel had left behind unopened. They stuff everything into the duffle bag on top of Abigail's letters and follow Jack home, all three oblivious to Abigail's lonely body on top of Johnny Daylight's grave.

With every strident step Jack, still carrying the pushchair, grows ever angrier with Rachel . . . Imagine abandoning a helpless baby? There could be no acceptable excuse for such thoughtless behaviour. He would have such words with that little madam when he got back. Ruthie had said she was getting above herself, well she has done it this time . . .

Relief and fear slosh around inside him like a night of whisky and beer, so that by the time he reaches home all his rational faculties have been subsumed by incandescent rage. Before Ruth can say anything in mitigation, Jack hands over Becky, and as a relieved Rachel runs towards her little sister Jack grabs her, turns her upside down and in hard syncopated slaps, beats her on her backside.

"Don't. You. Ever. Abandon. Your. Little. Sister. Again."

Ruth is desperate to intercede, but Jack will not be contradicted when it comes to laying the law down with the children, and besides, Jack is currently in a place unreachable.

Matthew and John arrive, awe struck to see their father beat their sister. He has never before raised a hand to her, and they each have mixed feelings: the goodness in them cannot watch the scene playing out and yet the badness inside says only 'at last'.

"He's beating the living daylights out of her," says John, still wondering if he should laugh or cry.

"Choked on her own vomit was what the policeman said. Who else's vomit would it be?" Jack asks, as Betsy pours him a very large Scotch.

Abigail, if you are here, if you are listening, I'm sorry. Truly. I didn't mean to tell you to fuck off. I didn't mean to wish you dead. I was a child. I barely understood what 'dead' meant.

You're making me confront something, something I am deeply ashamed of. I have never known what to do with the memory of your dead body. On one level it is like a scene from a particularly nasty movie, both compelling and repulsive. I did find you and it was vile, but not nearly as vile as my subsequent relief that you were dead. I can't imagine now being so afraid of anyone that their death is a relief. Imagine being that cold, that pragmatic, and underpinning all of that was the idea that I had caused it simply by willing it. It is a curse that you bring me to face myself, a curse. Yet here is the thing: the truth is, Abigail, worse than finding you dead was my father beating me.

Two

With the approaching dawn beginning to lighten the sky and the distant rattle of milk bottles, I give up my search for a shooting star and make my way back up the valley to my flat. Memories. Who are we without our memories? Even the ones that are false, those things we tell ourselves just to make our lives more bearable.

I remember the day, almost six weeks ago, when I first took my father to hospital as though it were happening now, as though something 'past' can be entirely real in the present.

A Foreign Land

"Rach? Can you come over? It's probably nothing but I want you to look at my leg."

"What's wrong with it?" Rachel shouted. Years of working without ear-defenders had reduced Jack's hearing by about eighty per cent, so he rarely used the telephone if he could help it, but this day was an exception – in more ways than one.

He'd hung up, frustrated. He'd never been a patient man. But he was worried, worried in a pretending-not-to-worry kind of way.

Rachel too, was worried; he rarely asked for anything. She got straight in her car and drove over to the bungalow. Although the mine had closed down years before, Jack and Ruth continued to live there, surrounded as they were by rusting decay and en-croaching land subsidence.

They were bound to stay; how could they leave the place where Rebecca had met her death? Rachel couldn't bear it, avoided visiting at all costs: inviting them to hers, meeting them in town, any excuse to stay away.

Ruth would remain there even if it meant being swallowed by the earth; she hated change of any de-scription, so moving was untenable. She was wor-ried about Jack though, and the fear she felt para-lysed her. He must have phoned Rachel because Ruth could not, suddenly mute.

When Rachel arrives Jack is in the kitchen. Waiting. His right leg is propped up on a chair. Rachel taps on the window as she passes and walks in through the open door. Jack wastes no time. "Wait 'til you see this." He stands up and starts to roll up his trouser leg. The normally loose brown fabric strains around his obviously swollen leg though. Breathless with the effort he gives up, unzips his fly, and slowly peels his trousers down. It's as if he's skinning a rabbit.

"Look! Would you look at that!" He's incredulous, like a child. Somehow this leg no longer belongs to him. The entire leg and foot is oedematous, blue-white human skin covering an elephant's leg. No sign of a knee or an ankle, and toes ready to burst, like plums, plump with September sun. His left leg appears skinny by comparison, but actually is still muscular and, at seventy-two, his flesh still fits his body. It doesn't hang from his bones, wrinkled and loose as old worn clothes, like some.

Close by, an abandoned boot lies on its side, yesterday's earth wedged between its tread, tongue hanging out like a dying dog, lace dispensed with and now coiling through Ruth's trembling fingers. She has tiptoed into the room and stands silent and erect in the corner.

Somewhere between the back door and the greenhouse there must be an impression. A footprint.

The TV is on. Daytime television, testifying to this being any old ordinary day; but this is far from ordinary. Rachel has never before seen her father ill. He had been bruised once she recalls: a mining accident, a runaway underground train which had trapped his arm. She remembers John and Matthew looking at Jack's arm, purple from wrist to shoulder. "F.A.B, Virgil. Return to base," John had said, bestowing Jack with honorary membership to the Thunderbirds. Harry had brought him home. Said something to Ruth about how the train might need a little repair work but would be fine, in the long run. They had all laughed. Why wouldn't they? Jack was a hero, like John Wayne or Superman; of course he could stop trains.

Jack is still a giant of a man; he has the build and thick neck of a prop-forward. But it isn't his size that impresses, it is his energy. All his strength lies around him in the space that he takes up and it runs through his veins at full flood. It is a palpable, emanating force, which you fall under like an electro-magnetic spell. He is invincible. Nothing could ever happen to him. He will outlive everyone. At least, this is how he seemed.

Jack and Rachel drive to City Hospital. It is a journey of paradox: silent and loud, fast and slow, long and short. They do not exchange one word between them, for they are carrying a passenger, a stranger, and they do not know if it is friend or foe.

Sitting in the crowded accident and emergency department, they are last in a very long line of people who are, it seems, much worse off. Jack is, if nothing else, sitting up. He is not cowering; he does not need to hold his head in place; or need to fold his arms across his chest just to stop his insides from spilling out.

Rachel fetches some tea from the vending machine. The tea is too hot and the plastic cup flimsy. It spills and scalds Jack's enormous hand, which is shaking uncontrollably. They both ignore this – the burn and the shaking. It is not easy to ignore – as he is never hurt, he never shakes.

They have been silenced and made powerless by events that have caught them looking the other way. As though they have, somehow, stepped off a cliff edge and impaled themselves on spikes.

Jack fixes Rachel with his clear blue eyes and says, "This would be funny if it wasn't so blasted laughable." His laugh, only half-heartedly begun, quickly retreats, back into a new place, somewhere deep inside him. Laughter, hiding. Rachel had never witnessed her father swallow laughter before. Never. Had anybody? Had Ruth? For Rachel this is a frighteningly absurd intimacy.

They sit limply, as if their bones have been removed, and like everyone else in the waiting area they are entirely drained of colour. Even their clothes seem to be fading as they sit there.

The artificial tropical plants are illuminated by false suns. The dry floors look wet. The staff, almost all dressed in white, march about wearing shoes that squeak, shoes that tap, and shoes so silent the staff must be floating above the ground.

Two men in white tunics and trousers have disposable masks, like small hammocks, underneath their chins; a place to rest their heads. They lope along, with their feet clad in white, rubber Wellingtons, their bodies protected in transparent, green, plastic aprons, and their hands latex-wrapped, swinging by their sides. On a mission.

In this strange world the people speak a somehow familiar yet incomprehensible language and the doctors are marked with purple half-moons beneath their eyes.

The department's head nurse is evidently working her last shift. After fifteen years of service on the front line she is giving up her buckles and badges and badgering for hard-earned retirement. Jack and Rachel glean all this through snatched comments from her can't-wait-to-step-into-your-silent-shoes sycophantic colleagues.

She is extremely short with an enormous bosom. She bustles and bosses with frightening efficiency, eyes constantly scanning. She doesn't miss a thing. She is an endangered species. An anachronism. Her face is round and pink, with kind eyes, sad though. She wears her hair confidently scraped back into an old-fashioned bun, just like Nurse Clemo. And because of this nebulous link with a safe past, neither Jack nor Rachel can take their gaze from her.

They wait and wait and wait. They manage to procure a wheelchair, which is a little too small. Jack is jammed into it, his broad shoulders hunched, his elbows drawn together.

"Put a glass box over you and you'd look like a

newsreader," Rachel commented.

"BBC or ITV?"

"What do you think?"

"ITV," he shrugs, smirking and resigned. And for a moment both of them disappear into the days before Winston Churchill's funeral when, finally, they had got a television set from Radio Rentals. To the days when Jack's children were happily content to wear a cardboard box over their heads and pretend to be tellies.

The offending leg, supported on a strut, kindly made soft with pillows, sticks out like a Dalek's antennae. Jack has suddenly become a cruel and unjust parody of himself. He's uncomfortable but feels it prudent if he doesn't complain.

They are, at last, moved from the waiting room into the treatment area. It is full and some of the cubicle curtains are not properly closed. They watch – compelled by inappropriate fascination – bits of other people's dramas, a hand, a head, a foot, an elbow, accompanied by disembodied voices, emotions being strangled. Hot body odours mixing, uneasily, with the smell of cleaning fluid.

There are people lying around on stretchers who do not have curtains at all; they are variously in pain, vomiting or bleeding.

Jack and Rachel simply wait in the wings. Wait for

their cue.

One young girl, who does have a curtain, is miscarrying. Jack and Rachel can see the nagging 'stand up, sit down' silhouette of her mother who will not let up with her interrogation to find out "How could this happen?"

Jack and Rachel exchange glances between themselves and the God of ceilings. Eventually, the young girl is rescued by the head nurse, who takes the mother away. They never see the mother again.

Finally, in the curtained cubicle the doctor speaks to them as if delivering a speech. "We think you have deep vein thrombosis. We will know for sure when the blood results come back. It's worrying that the thigh is also swollen; usually we expect the swelling to be just around the calf. Like I said, we will know more when the bloods come back. Of course, if it is deep vein thrombosis it can be treated with anti-coagulant therapy, Warfarin. You know? Rat poison." This amuses the doctor but seeing unresponsive faces she moves, swiftly, on. "We will have to admit you to the haematology ward. You'll need careful monitoring because of the risk of bleeding. Your blood pressure is high and we don't want anything untoward happening. Unfortunately there are no beds available at present."

Jack and Rachel are not given a chance to ask any

questions; the busy doctor has moved on to the next cubicle where a young boy has fractured his collarbone. Then it seems as though suddenly the cubicle curtains are billowing silks, that this is a desert land and they are Bedouin at the mercy of the elements.

Jack says, "This is a game of cat and mouse."

"Which are you?"

"The mouse. Most definitely the mouse."

Rachel thinks of next door's cat all that time ago and a shiver rips through her. She wants to vomit, but doesn't.

The doctor comes back, eventually. She is young and pretty and it dawns on Rachel that this is the reason why Jack is being so unusually cooperative.

The doctor has a sheaf of lab reports in her dainty manicured hands. "It's as I said, your blood is too thick and we'll need to thin it. How long have you been a diabetic?"

Jack and Rachel respond in unison: "A diabetic?" Their shock is not wasted on the doctor, but it is clear that she has no time for counselling so she ignores their obvious concerns and carries on. "The good news is we have a bed. All we need now is a porter. I'll see you on the ward later." And with that she is gone.

"Do you think if I applaud she'll come back and do an encore?" Jack is becoming angry and Rachel feels relieved. Negative emotion here is, she thinks, a good sign. Anger is good.

After what seems like an eternity the head nurse decides that they have suffered enough; she takes them to the ward herself.

Pushing from behind the wheelchair she can't see over Jack's head, so she cranes her head to the side. They are cheek to cheek, two strangers, the back of his head resting against her breasts. It is curiously intimate, a kind of silent conversation of fear and re-assurance: a trusting tango.

Rachel feels very sorry that the nurse is leaving, as though during the five hours in her department she has become inexplicably dependent upon her quiet strength, so much so that she can't imagine how the place will manage without her. How will they?

The trio follow the 'yellow line' which takes them to the wards; the green is for X-ray, blue for outpa-tients, and red for theatre. The lines are drawn along the floor and, to the uninitiated, they are a simple contemporary design. Ruth and Jack are grateful for this ball of golden thread to guide them through the labyrinth.

Rachel fears all that they are about to encounter, but pushes the feeling far back and down inside her body, into her kidneys. Not caring if it turns to stone.

She is also disconcerted when the journey takes

them past the mortuary, for it seems to Rachel to be worryingly close to the kitchens. Also, they appear to be heading in an opposite direction to everyone else and while Rachel feels suddenly clumsy in her body, the others seem to glide past, like angels smug with wisdom.

They arrive, at last, at the haematology ward. Rachel goes off to get a coffee, leaving Jack to say goodbye to the retiring nurse and get settled in.

Rachel finds the WRVS shop and sits with a large mug of frothy coffee and a slab of sponge cake. She is reminded of her Auntie Doris and the cakes she made. It troubles Rachel that the world would look at Doris and judge her by her size and not by her life, not see the heroine in her, not see that despite two of her children dying she somehow carried on. To the world Auntie Doris was fat and took up too much room. However, no amount of cake could have helped her recover from the death of her two boys. No amount of fat could ever shield a mother from a life with that sort of pain.

Rachel looks around the small café; lots of people are eating cake. Some are in their slippers and fluffy white dressing gowns and must have escaped from the near-by wards. It was strangely reassuring, and Rachel imagines her father doing the same in a few days' time, sneaking off with his mates for a sticky bun. How could he have diabetes and not know it?

She thinks of Ruth and of Harry, and of how worried they must be. In fact she thinks of everything except what is actually happening. She pushes her cake away and goes to the shop and buys Jack a paper so he can complete the crossword. He loves the cryptic crossword. He loves the way that answers can leap to mind instantly, or come after much deduction, and sometimes not come at all and have to be hunted out the following day to discover just how blindingly obvious they always were. But for Jack nothing is quite as satisfying as solving a 'smart ass clue': it is to do with recognising the cleverness of the compiler; it's to do with respect.

Rachel didn't bring Jack to the hospital expecting him to be admitted, so she also selects from the shelves a few choice toiletries, a bottle of sugar free squash and some sugar free mints, making a mental note to get him to see if they can sort out his terminal indigestion.

And on one level this all puts her back in absolute control; although this is new, and shocking and scary, she can concentrate her mind for a while, still herself.

Now I've had weeks of fear that won't be driven

away and it seems to have mingled with all the fear I have ever felt and I am drowning in it.

Adorable Becky floats up to the surface of my mind in ways that she hasn't for years, ways too tantalising to entertain, and I push her away like I have Abigail. But she insists – insists – on looking me in the eyes.

So I go over what happened to my father at the hospital; I play it over and over so as to re-write the end, in a way I can handle . . .

Paw Prints On Bread

Rachel makes her way back to the ward and pushes through the heavy double doors. Her attention is drawn to the television room, where the light from the TV flashes like lightning in the darkness and the theme music from a video of Inspector Morse blasts out. Rachel turns to look inside and to her horror sees her father plonked in front of the television, like a recalcitrant child. She rushes over and kneels down next to him. "Why aren't you tucked up in bed?"

"It's not quite ready yet. My lucky day. Think I'll get a lottery ticket." He attempts a smile, but Rachel knows it's for her benefit; he's miserable and ex-hausted. Not the simple exhaustion of a tired body either: the exhaustion of a tired soul.

On the table next to him is a jug of water and a

sandwich tightly wrapped in transparent film."Could you do me one favour and open that for me dharlin?"

Despite Rachel's nimble fingers and long nails she struggles with the wrapping, eventually biting into it and managing to liberate the suffocating sandwich. It is then that she notices the bread holding onto the shape of Jack's fingers, where he'd tried and failed to open it himself. He must be starving. She is enraged – enraged – because what would it have cost the person who brought these to spend two extra minutes helping her father to have his dinner? Of course she doesn't say anything. At least not out loud, but on the inside . . . The lazy bastards. The uncaring lazy bastards. Couldn't open a bastard sandwich . . .

"Dad, you're going to have to make a fuss; they'll not take any notice of you otherwise. Can't you pretend to writhe around in agony or something?"

Jack looks into Rachel's eyes and very simply says,

"But I am in agony". Rachel loses all control of her bottom lip and tears burn and stream down her cheeks, as if a world of shame was escaping.

It was in that moment, that defining moment, amidst transparent food wrap and Inspector Morse on the television that I had to face the terrible truth. The terrible fucking truth that my father, Jack Tangye, is every bit as vulnerable as everyone else. How blindly stupid have I been? He placed his big paw on the side of my face.

"Don't cry. I'll be alright . . . "

A Room Of His Own

Eventually, Jack is given a room of his own, off to the side, where it is quiet. He has his own TV and an en-suite bathroom. He has a drip placed in his arm and a bed cradle over his legs, lifting the weight of the bed linen from his painful leg.

The 'named' nurse, Debbie, is a petite, gorgeous, curly haired brunette with big brown eyes and a bubbly personality. "Your father will be fine with us; we'll see that he behaves himself."

Nurse Debbie is probably only about twenty-three, yet she smiles and winks at Jack in a flirtatious way that can't fail to make him feel like a man.

He smiles too. "Now you can't make a man go against his basic nature dhar-lin."

"You wouldn't want to be giving me any trouble

now . . . " Debbie laughs easily and tucks him in, in that proficient way that nurses seem born with. Then she plumps his pillows up enthusiastically, something she must have done countless times before, for countless people.

Rachel leans over and kisses him good night, as if this were any other night. She's attempting to make things appear normal. Except, normally, Jack and Ruth would stand together in the open door way and wave Rachel off: his right arm stretched up high, hand spread open, his left wrapped around her mother's shoulder.

"They will X-ray his vein tomorrow. The consultant will review him on the ward round in the afternoon. We'll work on getting his prothrombin time down. With any luck he'll be home ASAP." The charge nurse puts his hand on Rachel's shoulder. She says "good-night" and leaves.

The way the staff speak puzzles Rachel; it's almost like a foreign language you need to have command of to survive in the terrain. They deliver information in a pidgin kind of way; staccato facts rattled off at speed, with no explanations, no examples, and always as if they are just daring you to leap in with a question. Perhaps they are as afraid of questions as she is of answers? Whatever. They cannot remember what it must be like to be a visitor in their treacherous country.

Rachel steps outside the hospital main doors and is at once hit by the cold. She puts her left hand up to the place where the charge nurse touched her. She can still feel the firm grip of his warm hand. She finds it alarming how easily she can reach out for any thread to hold onto, no matter how tenuous it may be. She has a desperate need to hold on.

She inhales deeply, grateful for the fresh air. There's a slight breeze, but otherwise it is a clear autumnal night. She finds her car and looks back at the sprawling hospital buildings. A microcosmic city: all the windows lit up against the black sky, all life contained behind the towers of glass, every emotion being felt. She notices the smoke billowing out from the incinerator chimney, itself almost as tall as the tallest building. The fire in the furnace must be hot enough to soften steel.

Rachel wonders how the bed Jack now occupies came to be vacant. Would someone be discharged at this time of night? Did they pull the plug? Had they been waiting for a body to cool down sufficiently for it to be transferred to the mortuary? Rachel opts for someone discharging themselves, and then she realises that during all the times she has had occasion to roam through hospital corridors and sit by hospital beds she has never once seen a coffin or a covered corpse on a trolley. By which deceptive act do they manage this?

Rachel reaches her car and is dismayed to find a parking ticket. Perfect.

Dearest Johnny,

I write now from habit without hope that you will ever read what I have to say. I have been thinking about love. I can't bring myself to use the word 'infatuation' because it somehow belies the aspirational qualities of those wondrous emotions that have flooded my being since first we met. I have been pondering over whether our love is real? And have concluded that I will find truth in faith and then be free to trust. You see, Johnny, I do trust you, despite evidence to the contrary. I trust what we had to be real.

With love,

Abbie xx

I place Abigail's letter on the table next to the others. I could not walk back from the beach fast enough, such was my desire to find my old duffle bag and once again pore through her writing.

It's strange, I know, but I had this sudden idea that somewhere hidden between the lines of her fading ink I will find out what she wants.

However, I have only the few salvaged from the day of her dying. I can't be sure over what period of time the letters were written, none of them are dated and they, in turn, contradict one another . . .

Dearest Johnny,

The worst kind of lie is the black lie. The one you tell only to yourself. The one about love. The one about love conquering all. You see, Johnny, love has no need to conquer. Love is not to be bent, besought or bargained with. I am ashamed Johnny. I have tried to manipulate love and the more I grasped, the further away you slipped. Now I see that the people we love do not hand love to us on a golden platter. They inspire us to open our hearts and feel what is always there, our very own abundant supply of love.

I have trampled over the roads and pathways of our loving and I come to rest here in this strange place of knowing, where, at last, I realise that love is simply love: a power beyond will, which rests in my heart. I can give it away. I can receive it with gracious thanks. But I cannot take it. I cannot make you love me. And all my loving can't transform you into that which I want.

I can and do love you but I cannot expect anything in return. This love, Johnny, this unconditional love, is true love: imagine two hearts blossoming beneath this one sun.

I will not find this now with another but I rejoice that I have found it in my heart, because it cannot be taken from me and with it I am no longer lost. I walk in the light Johnny, and I bless our days.

With profound love,

Abbie xx

I read this one over and over. The image of Abigail's corpse is burned into my memory and it is so hard to see her "walking in the light". Her frail decrepit body beaten by a life that brought her misery. And yet as I stare at my memories of her she becomes a walking lie. She was so much more than she seemed and I am baffled at how this stranger has shaped my own life when all of my perceptions of her have been so wrong. A witch. A bag lady. A drunk. A woman. A daughter. A lover. A poet. An angel lifesaver?

How many personalities made up Abigail? I have to open my eyes. Abigail Daylight, like Granny Opie, is trying to tell me that I am blind. What could have happened that was so bad that I am unable to see it?

Unable to remember it? For as surely as gravity binds me to this earth, I am held by something.

Dress Rehearsal

A few days after Jack's admission to hospital he is wheeled down to X-ray where they take pictures of his vein. Rachel is left in his room, staring at the space that his bed took up. The blood pressure machine. The oxygen tubing. And the red call button that you hit hard and fast to summon the shock troops to re-start a broken heart. It's all suddenly revealed to her, in all its clinical starkness. And it makes everything so unbearably real. She wants to run away, like she had from Abigail's corpse. According to Jack, only cowards run away though, so Rachel sits alone with nothing better to do than rehearse how it feels to grieve.

Blackberry Jelly

As Rachel sits next to the hospital bed, Jack asleep with the relief of the X-ray being over, she finds herself awed by the forgiveness that exists between them, the full unconditional acceptance of all that is flawed in their humanness.

There is an invisible umbilical cord that requires a sharper instrument than a midwife's scalpel to separate them. He is the only person on this earth to whom she feels she never has to explain herself. Surely what they have between them, joining them, will survive death?

The door slammed open, waking Jack with a start. The consultant, in pinstripe suit, in tow with large shuffling entourage, enters the room. He is reading notes and peering at Jack over the top of his spectacles, like a nosey neighbour, standing on tiptoes to see over a fence. He listens with his head tilted to one side as the most junior doctor stutters out the blood results. He seems very young. Jack and Rachel are both at attention, every muscle stiffened, every ligament coiled as if poised on starting blocks and awaiting the shattering sound of a starting pistol.

And then . . .

"I suppose you wouldn't say no to going home?" He looks at Jack, and then back to the hieroglyphics, which tell the story of battles won and lost. Rachel thinks she must have misheard, but no, the consultant continues. "There's not much we can do for you here . . . that is, that your GP can't cope with . . . We still need your blood checked daily, so we can alter the amounts of Warfarin. That okay with you?"

"That's fine with me Doctor; I don't want to take up a bed un-"

The team turns, white coats parting, as the dark suit walks between them, a groom without his bride; and for a moment Rachel wonders if the stripes in his suit are bars that imprison him.

The young doctor just about had time to say, "I'll be back."

"That's a stroke of luck; you better ring your mother." Jack can't hide his excitement. He tries to stand up but his right leg is, if anything, more swollen than it was the previous day. "Don't go bothering about this; it'll go down in its own good time."

Rachel walks to the public phone, deeply uneasy about this sudden turn around. She had convinced herself that Jack was in serious trouble. But he can't be, can he? Why would they let him home?

Ruth weeps when Rachel tells her the news, and won't stop for a long time. By the time that Rachel returns to Jack he is lying on top of the bed, dressed. Except there is one missing shoe and a sock slit down one side, still strained around a fatted calf.

They wait for the doctor, watching rugby to pass the time. New Zealand are thrashing England at Twickenham. "I played on that pitch as a school boy," Jack comments, indifferently.

This is news to Rachel. Sure she knew he played Rugby, and that he played well enough to coach the Cornwall colts, but that he had competed on an international pitch . . . what had happened to that information? Where in her head were the family mythologies?

Neither of them see the junior doctor again. It is Nurse Debbie who brings the Warfarin tablets and a book in which to record the blood results and correct dosage, as well as other pills to balance the blood sugar. There is also a future appointment at the outpatient clinic. So there it is, 'a future', despite the fact that Jack's blood is slowly setting, like blackberry jelly . . .

Rachel's Wish Come True (1)

Rachel has Becky on reigns: they are going black-berry picking. They have two enamel milk jugs with them and Rachel is determined that they will return with both full to the top with fruit. It will please Jack – he'd use them for wine making – and Rachel was desperate now to placate him. Like a beaten dog crawling on her belly she would will him back to her. She will show him that she deserves his love again. That she can once more be trusted. Close-by to the bungalow (Rachel no longer allowed out of sight of the home) is a derelict building covered in brambles and heavily scented dog-roses. Part of the earth has been scorched, where people have tipped household rubbish and set fire to it.

A charred mattress with rusted springs sticking

out of it competes for space with the skeleton of an old sofa and a doorless fridge. But amongst this detritus grows an abundant crop of blackberries.

Very soon Rebecca's cheeks and chest are stained indigo. "For goodness sake, Bex, you're meant to pick them – not eat them!" Rachel picks Rebecca up and carries her to the old mattress and sits her down. "You stay there while I climb the wall – and don't eat anymore!"

Rachel clambers through the brambles, ignoring the barbs tugging at her clothes. Soon she is lost in her work and feeling quite pleased with herself. Suddenly there is the loud clang of an enamel jug hitting stone, followed by the resounding thump of a child hitting the ground, and then the long, drawn out silence of a scream before it finds its voice, and attached to that scream Rebecca's distinctive cry.

Rachel turns, her body made heavy, insides dry and desiccating as she looks upon Rebecca's blood-stained body, her small lacerated limbs flailing about her as she wildly stamps up and down begging to be picked up.

In one leap Rachel is off the wall and holding Rebecca's hot, sticky body in her arms, feeling her fear subside, her tears abate.

Upon closer inspection Rebecca bears no cuts at all; she'd simply dropped the jug of berries and then fallen onto them. Rachel cries with relief and then laughs so loudly that Rebecca laughs too.

Happy hysterical sisters. Rachel's wish come true.

•

Tasting The Earth

Much to Jack's annoyance he is wheeled in a chair to the main door of the hospital where Rachel meets him with the car. They have enormous difficulty fitting him into the passenger seat because his sticky-out-leg refuses to bend and all of the adrenalin that brought them here has been spent. Rachel is not only frustrated but angry; they were given no painkillers.

"I'm glad to be out of that place I can tell you,"Jack said grinning, as if he'd just escaped from Colditz. "Don't spare the horses."

It takes a good deal of grit and determination to get to his front door but he makes it; he probably would have crawled if necessary. He characterises illness as weakness, and it tears Rachel up to see him struggle. He uses her shoulder to support himself, squeezing her bones so tight she thinks they'll snap. But through this she feels his pain. She feels the heavy bursting flesh of a limb made hideous, a limb now capable of humiliation, embarrassing a body that was once lithe and strong. The body of a man who could tuck an oval ball underneath his arm and smash his way through a wall of men, a smile on his face, joy in his rampant heart, as he propelled himself up and over the white chalk line, flying through the air like a dancer, landing and sliding over wet turf, tasting the earth, scoring for the team, right between the posts. Smaller men, slower men, left tackling the air where his ankles had been.

Ruth has the kettle on and a sparkle in her tear-rimmed bright eyes: all is now well again in their world.

Rachel stays for a while and telephones each of her brothers to tell them the news, and then makes a call to the local surgery. She needs a GP visit, painkillers and a District nurse to come and take daily bloods – the simple instructions given by Nurse Debbie.

"Why can't your father come to the surgery? It is the weekend you know." The receptionist has a voice as bland as junket.

"Because he's just come out of hospital and he's in agony."

"They wouldn't have let him out if he was really

that ill."

"He can barely walk. We have tablets to thin his blood and tablets to balance his blood sugar, but no painkillers." Rachel wanted to say, "but no fucking painkillers", but some invisible power restrains her. Instead, she imagines biting into the woman's jugular, ripping the sinewy vessel from her flesh. "My father needs the doctor and the nurse in the morning," Rachel adds, and hangs up.

The force behind the receiver going down almost breaks the phone.

It's not love, nor is it the passion of love, which makes us angry, but fear. Honest to goodness fear. Hate is not love's opposite, fear is. Did you fear Johnny, Abigail? Fear all that he made you feel?

Dearest Johnny,

You did to me what you always do. You took me. And left. You will never understand the anger I felt, the humiliation. You betrayed all the potential of our loving. Forgive me, I dare to call it 'loving'. But of course you don't know about loving, you know only about 'using' and 'conquest'. I hate you. I hate your dishonesty. It may be the weapon you wield to shield yourself, but you damage people with it. Listen to this, Johnny, when you harm someone else it is like casting a stone into still waters; the ripples go to the shore and then return, they return and return and return until energy is spent and tranquillity restored. Until you know that you are worth loving, Johnny, you will never find peace. Until you know that you are worth forgiving, Johnny, you will never find peace. I struggle with these things daily, Johnny. I struggle with self-contempt.

A xx

I fold all of Abigail's letters and place them back into the duffle bag. I am suddenly tired of her. I did feel profoundly shocked by her death but I grew out of my childish idea that I had somehow made it happen. And truly, I did not give any of my attention to her at all – I pushed her away like an unwanted dream. And now, since dad's illness, she has resurrected. I wonder if that is exactly what Johnny did; pushed her away like an unwanted dream? Did he really go to his grave not knowing how much he was loved?

Dad had been home from hospital a week when I had my first nightmare . . .

Jack is lying in a hospital bed. He is diminished in size or the bed is much bigger. The bed appears to be floating in darkness. There is only Jack and the bed. He is lying back, nestled into the pillows, his arms lying next to him, palms turned up, the forefinger and thumb of each hand lightly touching, as if in meditation. He has a serene, blissful expression on his face. His eyes are closed. His body is swathed in white. He is dead.

I got up out of bed and paced up and down, not daring to disturb him or my mother at three in the morning. I walked to the beach and waited out the hours until dawn and the sprint home when at last I could call and hear my mother say, "He's all right darling, he's with me." Twice that's happened and it's the same dream, like a repeated acid trip doing my head in.

Now I make regular trips to the beach with or without a nightmare. In the vast endless ocean I find a degree of peace, something akin to that which Abigail found, not exactly a walking in the light but a sense of something greater.

Two weeks after dad's discharge we still did not have a proper diagnosis, but any fool could see his condition was deteriorating. The nurses were in attendance but they did not make much of it; they took the blood in their fast, efficient way, asked him if he was managing okay, and believed him when he said "yes".

I rang John and Mark in Australia, thinking that they should come home. John had family commitments, so it was agreed that Mark should come.

I met him at Redruth Railway Station: my baby brother, now in his thirties, almost six feet tall and tanned, stepped down from the train into a Cornish drizzle, wearing an Aussie hat. He had the sure footed lope of our father and the same blue eyes; it took my breath away.

I hadn't seen him for over ten years. When the mine closed down he'd joined John, who'd emigrated as a 'ten pound pomme' aged twenty-one, and was now well established in Adelaide.

From the platform I could see Carn Brea, the castle and monument shrouded in mist. Just below that lay St. Uny Church, where Abigail's and Johnny's bones finally came together, and while I helped Mark with his cases I reflected on how different Abigail's life may have been had Johnny stepped down from a train into her waiting arms.

Mark is naturally effervescent, in a Jack Tangye kind of way, talking about John and his family, about work, about his new girlfriend and then, it dawns, he is in love, and I think that this will make all things better, that he has brought with him optimism and happiness and that, if anything is to cure dad, it will be this, his youngest son.

It is 24 December 1999 and we drive through the dismal, dark streets of Redruth where Christmas lights and trees hang limply across the roads.

When we were children there was always a Santa grotto in the West End Drapery Stores, but times have changed.

"Mum hasn't put her tree up,"I say matter of factly.

"Is he as bad as that?"

"Worse, much worse."

The rest of the journey was made in silence. We had nothing to say.

Motherhood And Wifedom

Ruth stands beside the window peering out into the dark night; it was raining hard against the glass. She turned and looked at Jack, her handsome strong husband still in bed at 9am. He never lay in bed. He was always up: cooking his breakfast, reading his paper, and then out to the greenhouse or turning soil over in the vegetable plot.

Yet, here he was fast asleep and disappearing before her very eyes. How had he got so thin? How had he got so thin so fast? Some denial in her forces her head back towards the window. Surely he would recover. Jack could do anything if he set his mind to it.

Ruth used to love Christmas. It was the time she looked forward to most: buying the presents months in advance; hiding them away; always managing to get the children just what they wanted. She felt so blessed with her children; they never asked for much.

Rebecca's death changed all of that. In one dreadful day Ruth's world slipped on its axis and all that was once warm and soft became suddenly hard and brittle.

Ruth continued to buy Rebecca a small gift – a toy one year, a small piece of jewellery the next. And she would wrap it up, tenderly and beautifully. But she couldn't place it under the tree with the others; she had to keep it hidden in the dark, at the bottom of her wardrobe. Even now, after all these years, she might lay the table for seven, to then have to angrily correct her mistake before Jack saw it. They were two now. Just two.

She walked into the kitchen, filled the kettle and placed it on the hob. It took her a few seconds to realise she'd let the Aga go out. Again.

Some Christmas Day this was going to be. I'll sort it, nobody needs to know; it's still early. Mark had got in late. He wouldn't be up for ages. Poor boy. The look on his face when he saw his father – any wonder he went out for a drink. Bit like his father that way – loves his drink. He tried so hard to be brave and strong in front of Jack but his bottom lip quivered like he was five years old again and refusing to go to school. He could be so defiant; they all could. They get that from their father too, especially little Becky. The tantrums she'd have if she couldn't get her own way. That Christmas she'd refused to let Jack kill her favourite chicken. And he'd been feeding it up for weeks, but he backed down – had to; he could be so soft. I thought he'd kill her when a fox ate the blasted bird in the end, but he helped her to bury what was left, wooden cross and all; they put it next to Sputnik's grave…

As Ruth removes the ash can fine grey dust floats up and settles on her cheeks so that tracks of tears decorate her face with fine, white stripes.

Fatherhood And Husbanddom

Jack lay in his bed trying to use the bottle the nurse had left him. His leg was now so swollen he couldn't move it; it was too heavy. It meant he had to sleep through the night in one position and his backside was getting very sore. He'd started to get chest pains too; they shot through his lungs like hot arrows. But they were over in a second, and it didn't happen that often.

Some Christmas Day this was going to be. He would definitely get up today though. He'd wanted to yesterday, but somehow the time had just disappeared. He would get up today and try a bit of turkey. He'd see just how those scallywags would do without his expertise. Poor Ruthie can't do it all on her own.

He'd get up today. But first he'd just have a little sleep. He might even dream of Mark again. That would be grand . . .

Christmas Day

Christmas Day is an abject disaster. Jack had always cooked the roast: turkey, roast potatoes, roast parsnips, caramelised onions and red cabbage, Brussels sprouts with roasted chestnuts and steamed carrots and peas, all served with bread sauce, gravy and cranberries. Always followed by one of Ruth's Christmas puddings alight with brandy and served with clotted cream. Jack loved it, they all did. They wore paper hats, ate too much, drank too much and still had a mince pie. This was how Christmas had been every year until Rebecca had died. Following her death Christmas Day was exactly the same, except everyone's emptiness piled onto Rebecca's empty plate.

Matthew agreed to meet Rachel at the bungalow early

on Christmas morning and they would cook the dinner. Matthew's wife and children would join them later, picking up Harry on their way, so all that could be gathered would be and together they would all make this a special Christmas, regardless of how any of them felt. Nobody saying out loud that it might be their last Christmas with Jack. Last Christmas.

Rachel arrives before Matthew. Mark wasn't up, Jack was asleep and Ruth was in the kitchen. She was sitting in her dressing gown, grubby with ash. And she'd been crying. She hated Christmas.

Rachel went to the fridge, opened the door, and was so shocked by what she saw that she closed it up again, abruptly. Holding her hands over her mouth and nose she dared open it back up again, slower this time. On the middle shelf sat a defrosted turkey, covered in a thick black mould, a mould that had spread throughout the fridge, contaminating all the other food and drink, and covering all the white surfaces. It stank. It made her stomach churn. Mark entered the room. "What's up?"

"The turkey's off!"

Mark steps forward, opens the door and closes it again, at speed. "Streuth, it is flaming off."

They start to laugh, a combination of things: not least his pseudo-Australian accent but just gallows humour that has Rachel doubled over and tears springing into

Mark's eyes. They laugh so much it hurts.

Ruth looks at her children-adults, at first in horror, and then too she is laughing, helplessly laughing, all her pain pouring out of her. She rubs her face and smears of soot spread black warrior markings over her pink skin. Her white hair foppishly flopping over her forehead.

Matthew steps, cautiously, into this madness, always the serious, controlled one.

"What's up with you lot?" Then looking at Ruth, "What have you done to your face?"

In unison, Rachel and Mark manage to point at the fridge and say, "The turkey's off," before they collapse again.

Slightly irritated, Matthew opens the door, and like those before him, immediately closes it. He hugs his belly, his six-foot-four-inch frame bent in the middle. Mark and Rachel can tell he doesn't know whether to laugh or vomit; he's inherited Ruth's sensitive stomach. Seeing his normally cool demeanour rupture just makes them laugh all the more.

Later that morning Mark and Matthew carry the fridge on their shoulders to the nearby dump and ruthlessly abandon it and its contents.

Christmas lunch is canned tuna fish and chips. Harry tries his best. "That was lovely, Ruth – will you join me in a bit of port?"

"No thank you, Harry."

"One day you'll answer me 'yes' and I'll die of fright."

"I'll have some." Mark holds his glass out and Harry pours with a trembling hand. Rachel looks from Ruth to Harry and somehow they both appear to be ever-darkening shadows in the diminishing light of Jack and she feels that way too, as though her heart is being scrunched up like one of Abigail's letters. All this 'normality' being acted out, while Jack sleeps upstairs, sleeps away his last Christmas.

Matthew produces some Christmas crackers and they all pull them apart, popping on to their heads the coloured tissue paper crowns inside. This seems fitting, since the entire world seems suddenly made of paper. They, all of them, try to make some effort to give Matthew's children, Jade and Sam, a good time. They'd thought it 'cool' to have chips for Christmas dinner. They each take it in turns to read the jokes from the crackers, but the print is too small for Rachel, who has to reach for Jack's glasses on the sideboard by the phone, and Matthew looks at her and says, "Good God, you look just like Abigail Daylight."

I don't know what came over me: I suddenly snapped. I stood up too quickly, knocking my chair over, and yelled at him. "What do you know about Abigail? She may have been a source of ridicule to you and John but ... but ... "I burst into tears and fled, feeling rather stupid.

When I'd calmed down I went in to see dad; he'd refused lunch. "I knew you wouldn't manage the turkey without me," he said, the first hint of humour I'd seen in a while.

"Do you want to get up dad? I'll help you."

I was appalled at how much weight had dropped from him. We struggled but eventually I wrapped a towel around his back and under his arms and just pulled. He came to a standing position, which made him very dizzy. But once lowered into the armchair he was happy – he'd achieved something.

His voice was quiet, as though there was no breath in his lungs. "I'm not going to make this one," he said, like a bullet-ridden cowboy.

I wept helplessly. "It doesn't look good."

"Don't cry. When a man's got to go, a man's got to go."

He had no strength left to hold me.

So here I am, as usual, walking on the beach in the middle of the night, wishing for all the world that I am in fact tucked up in bed. Wishing that Christmas Day had been but a dream.

The gulls are silent now, nestled in the cliffs, blissfully sleeping. But thinking of gulls brings to mind a memory that has me laughing out loud. Out loud. Alone on the beach at four in the morning. Me with my madness, seeking a voice.

Discombobulating

Rachel is eleven years old. She's walking home from school. At the left turn that will take her up a bumpy lane, past the factory and onto the footpath across the fields to home she finds a seagull. It is fast asleep and perfect, not a smudge of dirt on its white and slate-grey feathers. It doesn't struggle as she carefully picks it up. She can feel its fine brittle bones beneath the soft feathers and she simply wants to take it home and love it.

Jack looks out from behind his newspaper. "Take that out of the kitchen Rachel! You don't know where it's been."

"Shhh! It's sleeping."

Jack laughs. "Asleep, is it? The sleep of the dead more like."

"It's not dead!" Rachel is horrified.

"How jolly discombobulating."Jack, smiling, gets up and takes the bird.

"That's not a real word."Rachel is trying not to laugh because she doesn't want any whimsical distractions to come between her and the gull, but she loves the word, struggles with it, like chewing a sweet, sticky toffee, dis-com-bob-u-lat-ing.

She follows Jack outside. He is buoyant – anything might happen. They reach a gap in the garden hedge through which they enter the adjacent field. Jack has his vegetables growing in this corner. The rest is lush meadow. He holds the seagull by its legs, and then, like a discus thrower, swings the bird three times around his head before letting go."If it takes off we'll know it's not dead,"he says triumphantly.

Rachel is struck dumb by his actions. The bird flies at first, arching over the long grass, but then, in fast falling somersaults, crash lands, hard on the ground – in a crumpled heap of broken, imperfect wings.

Rachel hits her father so hard it hurts her hands. Jack is split wide open with laughter, filling the field with glee.

I wish I realised it then, as the sting on my hand subsided, that it's not possible to hurt someone you love without also hurting yourself.

I feel so cold that all I want to do is lie down and sleep,

lie down and die, and let a stronger part of me continue telling my story, continue making it up as they go along …

Three

A Stronger Part of Rachel Making it up as She Goes Along

Rachel climbs the steep path through the valley, walking alongside the stream, which is coursing its way to the sea with such a winter force that every now and then white water suddenly spills onto the land, washing over the stones and puddling the pathway.

Sharp branches stripped bare of leaves hang low in the early mist, catching her hair and occasionally just missing her eyes. Scratches are good though; they make her feel something. Pain.

She is consumed by a dread, the dreadful truth that Abigail's ghost cannot help her father. Arriving at the flat she could hear the telephone ringing; she could hear it before she walked through the garden gate, before her key slid into the lock. She's heard it in the silence of her worries for weeks, but this time it's real, this time it's bad.

Her mother is incoherent. Rachel replaces the receiver and drives the fifteen miles in some sort of hinterland between this universe and another, everything around her made suddenly surreal.

Somehow she is out of the car and standing next to her father's bed. Jack is pale blue, like a drying clay sculpture. He doesn't move – he doesn't move – but there is a small breath tentatively trying to enter the top of his lungs.

Ruth is standing in her dirty, dressing gown. Another statue, she's pinned up against the wall, nailed there by fear.

Rachel goes to the phone. She has to find her voice. But large hands are wrapping around her throat, squeezing tightly.

"Which service please?" An utterly calm, disembodied voice coaxes all the essential information out of Rachel. Rachel responds in a quivery but controlled manner, part of her denying that anything is wrong, part of her filled with foolish hope, and part of her looking at the photographs of Rebecca which litter the top of the sideboard. Rebecca holding her pet rooster, Mr. Peggoty. Rebecca holding her prize chicken, Ginger. Rebecca winning a race at school. Rebecca sitting in her pushchair: Rachel, John, Matthew and Mark kneeling around her.

Rachel puts the phone down and opens the sideboard drawer and lifts out a small wooden box. It contains other mementoes: a silver bangle, a Sunday School picture Bible, Rebecca's death certificate and a newspaper cutting with the headline: SEARCH FOR MISSING GIRL ENDS IN TRAGEDY. Another: INQUEST RECORDS A VERDICT OF ACCIDENTAL DEATH. Rachel slams the box closed. Ruth is looking at her. Rachel looks back at her mother, but cannot hold the gaze (with her Granny Opie eyes, needing to look away to hide the truth). Rachel has seen this look before: hatred. Hatred in her mother's eyes. Mother to daughter, daughter to mother. Between these two, love, love and something else, unspoken. Something deeper than Dolcoath.

"Where's Mark?"

"At your brother's."

"Phone them. I've got to meet the ambulance; they'll never find us. Don't forget Harry."

Rachel is caught then, caught in indecision. Should she go back to Jack? Should she meet the ambulance? Should she hug her mother? Should she find a place in which to sleep?

She's not qualified. She's not responsible.

Fade To Grey (2)

Rachel expected the ambulance to go very fast. To speed, like her racing heart, to take her father safely into the emergency room where the efficient but compassionate head nurse would cradle him to her bosom and he would be replenished, nurtured back to wellness.

Instead, with Rachel's car, seemingly towed behind like an AA rescue, they manage a top speed of thirty miles per hour. They do not take the right turn to Truro where the major accident and emergency department is but the left one, towards Penzance. Towards a smaller hospital, one of less critical mass.

Rachel grips the steering wheel tight. He's still alive. He must be still alive. He would not leave without saying goodbye. He would have his last word.

The closer they get, the worse the weather becomes; torrential rain starts up and occasional hailstones bombard the windscreen, until finally they arrive on the outskirts of town in the midst of a raging storm. It's still dark, the streetlights are reflecting off the wet roads, and waves are crashing over the sea defences and sweeping up a gully and spilling onto the main road just before the railway station. The sea front must be awash with seaweed and pebbles.

It's surreal. All of it. Rachel can't stop thinking that ambulances do not travel at thirty miles an hour when they have their blue lights flashing on and why is this one deathly silent? Where are the sirens screaming to get out of the way?

The ambulance takes the by-pass which is higher up, and from here the entire town is made small and model like, turned into an animated postcard.

The ambulance goes straight into the emergency bay, but there is no parking space for Rachel. Desperately, she circles the small car park twice before realising that it is no use and will be no use, and forced back out onto the road where pedestrians with their makeshift newspaper umbrellas and tilted walks frustratingly impede her progress.

A loud blasting horn breaks her concentration, and then she notices that she is the one slamming hard on the horn, and through this chaos she clearly sees a parking space, just opposite the hospital. A space has opened up for her, and for a moment the rain has stopped.

She meets the ambulance crew who are returning to the ambulance with an empty stretcher. "We had to take it slow – your dad wasn't feeling too good. He's perked up now he's had some oxygen." The chirpy men in green saunter off. Job done.

Not feeling too good, is that all?

In this hospital there are no painted lines to follow; instead Rachel must read the signs. Eventually she finds her father.

Jack had been admitted straight onto a ward, and she pulls open the floral print curtains which surround his bed and watches as a doctor finishes injecting something into the intravenous infusion which is sited in the back of Jack's left hand. A nursing assistant is busy clearing away paper and plastic packaging which are lying on top of him. He has an oxygen mask covering his mouth and nose, which is attached by elastic; it stretches across his cheeks, pinching the flesh, so that he has four cheeks now, four pink cheeks.

Jack opens his eyes and glints at Rachel who hasn't dared to move closer. She puts her hand up to her mouth.

She must be brave, like him.

Rachel steps forward and kisses him on his forehead. His eyes are amazingly clear: the whites still white, not rheumy like Harry's or her mother's. A nurse joins them. He has a small cardboard tray in his hand, the kind they use to put chips in. He also has a very long ponytail tied back with a postman's rubber band. His hairline is receding and the tip of the tail is very thin. Rat like. But he is pleasant, friendly, kind and reassuring. Perfect. He would not leave someone struggling to remove food wrap from a sandwich.

"Hello Mr. Tangye. I've got to give you this small injection; it's called Heparin. It'll help thin your blood." He lifts up Jack's pyjama jacket. "You haven't got much flesh have you? I wish my stomach was that flat." He pats his beer gut. He gives the injection quickly while the doctor shines a torch light into Jack's eyes. Rachel stares at Jack's belly and is shocked to see how hard it has become. Where has all the softness gone?

"We think you've had a pulmonary embolism Mr. Tangye. You're a lucky man and you should feel better very soon. Can I just look at this stomach of yours?" The doctor palpates Jack's abdomen, making small sounds like heartbeats with two fingers of each hand. Then he starts to press with the flat of his hand and once over the lower left side Jack cries out. The doctor, concerned, looks up at Jack, whose new pink cheeks rapidly fade to grey.

"I'm sorry. I'm going to get them to take a chest X-ray and get a scan of this stomach of yours. There's something not quite right here and it may be why that leg of yours is swollen."

Jack's eyes are shut; he is trying to control the pain. He can't hear the doctor because vanity won't allow him to wear his hearing aid, and besides he doesn't care about much anymore; he's had enough.

The doctor addresses Rachel, who is still reeling from Jack's scream. She has never heard him cry out in pain before, or, had she? Something inside her is stirring. An echo.

"That injection I gave your father is morphine. He'll drift in and out for a while . . . Shall we have a word?" He steps towards the curtains and holds them back for Rachel. She is also drifting in and out, overwhelmed by vanquished hopes.

They walk out of the six-bedded bay and into the long corridor. He invites her to sit down with him. There aren't any chairs in the vicinity though. She settles on a set of weighing scales; he chooses an abandoned wheelchair. It's too big for him. "Your father has had a massive pulmonary embolism. That's a blood clot that is blocking the blood supply to his lungs. Of course it's compromising his entire system, and it's also likely that something in his abdomen is pressing against the vein that drains his leg and this could be why his leg is so swollen." He pauses.

Rachel is trying to hide the fear in her, trying to grapple with this information. "But he'll get better?"

"It's possible that he could have another embolism."

"But you can cure that?"

"It's also very likely that the problem in his abdomen is some kind of growth. Some kind of tumour."

Rachel tries to arrest the tears that are flowing down her nose. Like a child she uses her sleeve to wipe away her distress.

"What are you saying?"

"Your father is a very poorly man. Very sick indeed."

Rachel becomes angry, forceful. "Can he recover?"

"I would say that his condition is critical. I can't promise."

"Can't promise! I need more than a promise. Is my father dying? Are you telling me that he is dying?"

"I will know more when we have the X-ray and scan results. He is very frail . . . "

Jack Tangye cannot be frail.

"It is unlikely, in my opinion, that he will recover."

Rachel is sobbing now, helpless. Then from somewhere she finds her father's courage and manages to force the issue, to find the truth. "Is. My. Father. Dying? For fuck's sake. Say it!"

"Yes. I believe your father is dying." The doctor sighs audibly, suddenly disabled by the limitations of his profession.

And so the scales upon which Rachel now sits tip heavily from love to grief and she enters into the silent world, which surrounds the dying, a world which is neither here nor there.

Fey Charm

In the West Cornwall hospital the X-ray machine comes to Jack, a futuristic robot on wheels with the capability of seeing through people, of illuminating their weak spots, of predicting bleak futures. It is pushed by a slightly built radiographer who has about her a fey charm, something other-worldly, elfin. "My name is Rebecca," she says. "I'm going to take a picture of your chest and then I'm going to do an ultrasound scan of your belly." She smiles at Jack as if he were normal, as if dying was an everyday thing.

"Rebecca – that's a grand name," he says, drawing from her some strength and comfort. "Do they ever call you Becky?"

"Yes they do, and they call me Bex too. I like that, it's naughty; it rhymes with 'sex'." She giggles, suddenly coquettish, and Jack laughs a little in response. But it hurts, so he returns to his dreams.

Rachel has practical concerns. She has to stand up from the scales and walk to the telephone to call her mother . . .

"No Mum. Listen. He's in Penzance Hospital. He's really very sick. Get Mark to bring you down straight away."

"It can't be so bad if he's in Penzance. You stay with him today. We'll come tomorrow. After he's had a rest."

"Is Mark there? Let me speak to him."

"I don't know where he is. He was here."

"Mum. Please. Please understand. Dad may not be here tomorrow."

"So they're sending him to Truro tomorrow? Okay dear, we'll go up then."

"No! Get Mark. Forget it! I'll phone Matt."

Of course Rachel wanted to be the gracious daughter; she wanted to break the devastating news as gently as possible. It was not her intention to slam the phone down on her mother, to slam the phone down on someone who was breaking up inside.

For Ruth, the idea of losing Jack was simply untenable; she had his room to clean. She needed to freshen it up for his return.

Diminishing Screams

Mark and Matthew had hired a power washer. They emptied the contents of the fridge onto a dumped mattress, covered the lot in petrol, and then set light to it. And, despite the weather, it was burning. Then they fixed together two garden hosepipes and were now taking it in turns with the jet to erase Christmas Day and all the mould from the inside of the fridge, in case it was a health hazard.

They were soaked through, each, accidentally, aiming the jet at the other and laughing. The fridge was spotless: no sign of rot. They took it back to the garage where it could be stored away safely.

Matthew hadn't slept because of it; he kept seeing a young child, a girl, fall into it, and the door slamming shut on her, where her diminishing screams would,

177

forever, go unheard.

Ruth opened the back door to them; and suddenly they were John and Matthew returned from the quarry to tell her that Rachel might have drowned. "Is Rachel all right?"

"Are you all right?" Matthew asked.

"I'm a silly woman, look at the pair of you; you just took me right back to that day Rebecca was saved by Abigail."

"You are a silly woman; that was Rachel – not Rebecca. And it was me and John, this one was still in nappies."

"Make us a cuppa Ma, it's freezing."

Mark is trembling with cold, but invigorated. He'd been grateful for the night at Matt's, had forgotten how grey the winters were in Britain. He needed the optimism of his nephew and niece, Sam and Jade, because the thing he'd flown across the world to witness, the thing that above the clouds had not seemed real, had become real the first moment that he had seen Jack. There was no question. His father was dying. He would have to bear it. They would all have to.

Neither Here Nor There

Rachel sits in the high-backed vinyl chair next to the bed. She is between Jack and the window, between Jack and the world. He appears much better; the morphine has worked its magic and he is pain free, and his colour has returned to normal, and now he can have the oxygen if he wants it, so for the moment the oxygen mask hangs above the bed, tangled in the tinsel of a Christmas decoration.

Ponytail nurse has suggested that they keep the curtains drawn so that they may have a bit of peace. An illusion of privacy.

Jack wakes and is suddenly very bright. "You still here?"

Rachel leaps from her mindless reverie. "Blimey you frightened me!"

Jack is visibly pleased; he has not lost all of his power.

"Thought I'd hang around. I still haven't been able to get hold of Mark or Matthew and I tried talking to Mum but you know how she gets."

"I'm really worried about your mother." Jack is serious. He's wanted to say something for ages but has been holding back, thinking, hoping, praying, that Ruthie was just going through some phase; but, no, there was no ignoring it, she was getting worse. She was going to the shops and not getting anything on the list. She was forgetting to stoke the fire, most of the time. And she was putting tea bags straight into the kettle. He'd chuckled the first time she had done that, it had an admirable efficiency about it, cutting out the middle man, so to speak. And she'd smacked his ass . . . she was a good woman. None of these things amounted to much on their own, but viewed in the round . . .

"She's worried sick about you."

"It's more than that Rach . . . " They let this hang between them; it was enough to say it out loud. Rachel nods at him. He can rest now. Ruthie will be looked after, she will be watched over.

After a while Jack says, "You know cancer really is the damnedest, most stupid, thing on this earth."

Rachel shakes her head and smiles at this wonderful man."What do you mean?"

"Well think about it. It's killing me, so in the end it will kill itself. Must be a metaphor for something."

Rachel loves these conversations with him, loves the side roads they travel on together.

She thinks immediately of Abigail.

"Obsessive love. It's a metaphor for obsessive love."

"What would you know about obsessive love? Any love come to that?"

"Don't! Don't say things like that to me." Rachel is cut deeply in a way that only Jack can manage. "Dying doesn't give you the right to trample on me . . . "

"Don't cry Rachel. I'm sorry. I worry about you. You're so defended. You deserve more than a lonely life. You're missing . . . " He changes tack. "Sorry, go on then, you tell me about obsessive love."

A hollow space opens up between them and they each fill this with jumbled ribbons of regret. After a while Rachel continues.

"Well as a matter of fact I was referring to Abigail Daylight. Obsessive love killed her."

"She wasn't right in the head that one."

"That's a bit hard; you must have read her letters. Imagine dying on your lover's grave like that."

"Oh, Rachel! Will you ever grow out of these romantic flights of fancy? She didn't die on her lover's grave!"

"She did! You know she did! You must remember! I

found her and you half-killed me. You can't forget that."

Jack sighs heavily. Of course he couldn't forget. Hadn't he had to live with it: beating his daughter, acting first, asking questions later? Yes he remembered. He remembered the look she'd given him, all of ten years old and some irrepressible spirit in her still able to wither him, a grown man. Any wonder he got pissed that night. She's a caution this one; if I'd another life I still wouldn't understand her.

He takes a deep breath.

"It's okay, dad, we're okay."

"No. I want to tell you something; there's only Harry knows, the rest are all dead now. That waster Johnny didn't die. We buried a pile of sand."

Rachel holds onto the arms of the chair as if tectonic plates were causing the earth to shift.

Jack continues. "Her father, Arthur Dean, was beside himself with worry. He could see his daughter slipping away from him the moment that that geek left town. He thought if he killed him off she would re-find herself. Of course the poor girl only got worse."

"But that can't be . . . That can't happen."

"I'm telling you Rachel. She died on an empty grave."

"But you need a death certificate . . . a registrar . . . a funeral for Christ's sake."

"What are you getting so worked up about? Calm down and let me tell you. You only need a death certificate when you're registering a death; there was no death, no body, just sand bags. Daylight was leaving anyway so Arthur Dean paid him to leave his daughter alone and never come back. I'm telling you, his grubby little hands grabbed that money as quick as you like. Later, when it was clear the poor lovesick-lamb wasn't going to recover until Daylight came back to her, Dean paid the undertaker – I dare say a handsome sum – to bring him back. The vicar took funds for the chapel, well at least that's what he said. Besides, they did think they were doing the right thing. You look in the church records – there's no burial of a Johnny Daylight. The plot was bought by Arthur Dean for his family. The undertaker put the coffin on a train at Truro and we took it off at Redruth."

"I can't believe it. I can't believe a man would be so cruel to his daughter. I can't believe you would collude in such a thing."

"Good grief Rachel. What's it to you? We thought we were doing the right thing. We didn't have counselling in those days, you know. Nobody knew how to help Abigail. She wasn't reachable. I'm telling you, Daylight was a waste of space. He didn't care one bit for that wretch of a girl. He tupped her and left."

"You're getting angry."

"Because you're getting so upset. If he loved her he would have come back. He would at least have sent her a letter or a miner's broach. You know the one good thing that woman did was to save your little life. Do you think I haven't been on my knees thanking God and her for that? Sometimes I think she was born just to do that, just to save you. We make mistakes Rachel; we make mistakes with our children." Jack is weeping now, weeping for all the mistakes in his life. "We have to forgive ourselves Rachel."

Rachel is in such turmoil she's hardly listening, but seeing his tears she softens.

"And how much did Arthur Dean pay you?"

Jack smiles. "He bought me a pint."

For some reason they both laugh at this, friends again. "Arthur Dean wasn't everyone's favourite man, but he was a fair man. If he hadn't been the mine captain we may have been mates, but he let us have the bungalow as God knows we needed it as we had that at the same rent as Number Two."

Rachel leans back in her chair, energy spent, trying to fathom all this new information. She could hardly believe it. An entire village had attended a funeral of sandbags. Supposing Johnny had returned . . . what then? She'd forgotten about the idea of miners' broaches; they were handmade bits of jewellery that miners fashioned out of the spoils of their work and sent home to their loved ones. Indeed, hadn't she watched Harry make her a tin skull and crossbones using tin smelted in his fire and poured into a plastic mould rescued from a cereal packet? One of the bones had fallen off because the tin had been too soft. Where on earth was that now?

"Will you let me sleep?" Exhausted, Jack closes his eyes.

"I'll go and phone Mum."

Clinging to the uncertainty clenched in her empty fists, Rachel makes her way to the nurse's station. Poor Abigail; Johnny really hadn't loved her. Johnny could still be alive and not know about the mess he had left behind . . . Hurricane Johnny.

Is this why you're here, Abigail? To understand your past? To share your bewilderment? How can I help you? I don't know what to do or say.

N F R

Harry, Matthew, Mark, Ruth and Rachel sit around Jack's bed. He's wearing the oxygen mask. The doctor had been right; he'd had another embolism. Alone, when Rachel had gone to the phone, he was gripped with such a pain he was sure it was the end of him. The words shouted loudly from behind his curtains: "Fuck Jesus." Words he did not intend in that order, and definitely not in the same sentence, brought Ponytail nurse to his side. "You could try using the bell Jack." Then, appreciating Jack's condition, he instantly switched from comic to professional. "It's okay mate, I'll get the doctor. You'll be all right; it's the same as before." He presses the call bell three times and another nurse comes running. Ponytail nurse has replaced the oxygen mask. "We need the doc."

The other nurse leaves and very soon Jack has another morphine injection. When Rachel returns, the drama is over, but the doctor needs a word. So they return to their seats in the corridor. This time it is she who is disabled and he who is weighing himself. Why are there no chairs?

"I have to ask if you want your father to be resuscitated?"

"What?"

"I'm sorry. The law requires that we resuscitate anyone who is newly admitted unless we have permission from the next of kin not to."

"But you said he was dying ... And now you're saying ... What are you saying?"

"I know this is very difficult but we have rules in place that are designed around generalities. To get to specifics means asking questions of the next of kin."

"Would he survive resuscitation? I mean, is he fit enough to live longer?"

"He might. Unlikely – but he might."

"And then what? I mean ... what if he did survive? He has to die all over again?"

"He'd be transferred to intensive care. He might get another day, an hour, a week. I can't tell you how long. But in all probability he would never regain consciousness."

"I am not qualified for this. You're making me responsible . . . My father is either living or he's not . . . You're the doctor."

The doctor is silent; he has learned to be patient in these situations.

"Leave him alone. Please just leave him alone."

"You have to sign this form. I'm really sorry. It's the world we live in."

He could advise her to discuss it with other members of the family, but there may not be time for that. He doesn't want to handle another pointless resuscitation. And they always happen at some ungodly hour. Besides, the man is beat. Whichever way you look at it, the man is beat.

Light Relief

Meanwhile, Jack is using up the last of his memories. He's recalling Rachel at about eight, sitting at the kitchen table with her head so close to the table top her nose is almost touching it.

"What on earth are you doing Rachel?"

"I'm staring!"

"Staring at what?" asks Jack.

"I'm looking for the light. You said light was everywhere, even in the colour black."

Jack laughs. "Do you think the light could be in the heart of the man who made the table? Have you thought about that?"

Rachel looks up at Jack with such a look of supreme condescension that he laughs louder.

"I'm glad you've found something to smile about?" The doctor pulls up a chair and sits next to Jack.

"Must be that stuff you gave me doc, I was remembering when Rachel was small."

"Your daughter?" The doctor loosens his collar and tie. "I've just been speaking to her."

"She didn't grab you by the throat and hoist you up the wall did she?"

"Metaphorically . . . I'm afraid I didn't have any good news for her . . . "

"No need to go on. I know I'm done for."

"The thing is, we could take a biopsy, but looking at the blood results and the scans, I'm not sure there's any virtue in putting you through it . . . "

"Nah. Leave me be. That's best."

"I can get the nurses to organise a chaplain or priest . . . "

"Nah, God will either take me or he won't . . . and there's an end to it."

"My mate Geoff Powell said to me once 'Well, Christ wasn't a Christian, was he?' It made me think about him, Jesus I mean, made me think he was a free-thinking radical, a bit of a maverick. I liked him after that."

Jack laughs. "I suppose Buddha wasn't a Buddhist neither. I must tell that one to Rachel, she'd like that."

"Can I get you anything?"

"I'll have another shot of that morphine. Never touched drugs in me life before, but may as well enjoy myself before I go."

The doctor leaves and Jack closes his tired eyes . . .

. . . I must tell Rachel. I must tell Rachel to forgive herself. And then his memory goes over it again, over and over that dreadful day.

That Dreadful Day (1)

Jack and Ruth go into Rachel's bedroom to wake her up. She seems to be in a deep sleep. John, Matthew and Mark are all sobbing. Their grief is muffled by two thick walls and a hallway, but Rachel hears it. She jolts and sits up straight, petrified.

"Rachel, Becky has had an accident. Rachel, Rebecca died. In our arms. This morning." Jack and Ruth agreed how they would tell their children. Jack had rehearsed it over and over and in so doing brought the truth sharply into focus. Now he numbly delivered the words while Ruth stood behind him grabbing hold of his knitted pullover.

Rachel puts her hands over her ears, shuts her eyes and screams. "No! No! No!" She leaps from her bed and runs into the toilet, leaving Jack and Ruth to listen to her retching. Then looking down, Jack notices the mud on Rachel's sheets and the small phrase 'mud sticks' swims in and out of his mind as a chilling idea creeps up his spine and enters his head. He turns his wife around and leads her through the door, closing it behind them. He prays Ruth didn't notice.

Goodbye

Jack's family are gathered around his bed, each of them knowing that this could be goodbye. Any day soon, any minute, any hour, could be goodbye. Jack has no tolerance for this at all and they are not there long before he says very firmly, "Thank you all for coming. I love you all." He shuts his eyes and all of them know that they have to leave. He can bear anything, has borne so much, but he can't think of goodbye and in truth neither can they. So with this mutual respect flowing into the streams of their futures, they each silently go forward and kiss him. Goodbye.

Ruth is supported out of the hospital by her two sons. Harry follows, trance like. He has aged today. They all have. Rachel stays behind, listening to the rain beating at the window and the distant rumble of thunder as the night grows darker.

Why did she become so angry at Jack? Why did she make him angry? Bloody Abigail.

Soon, despite the uncomfortable chair, Rachel joins Jack in sleep. Her head rests on the bare wooden arm, her legs are curled beneath her, and she's clenching her father's dressing gown, wrapped around her for warmth . . .

It is four in the morning. Jack lies still in his hospital bed. He is diminished in size or the bed is suddenly much bigger. The bed is floating in darkness: my Dad and the bed. He is lying back nestled into the pillows, his arms lying next to him, the thumb and forefinger of each hand lightly touching, as if in meditation. He has a serene, blissful expression on his face. His eyes are closed. His body is swathed in white. Jack has let go of Jack. He is dead. Rachel wakes with a shock from her nightmare . . .

Jack is prodding Rachel's leg and taking his oxygen mask off. His voice is so small she can hardly hear him. "Rachel . . . forgive . . . forgive . . . Becky . . . " Jack's last exhalation gathers behind his cheeks, and then slowly escapes through his closed lips, making a sweet sound of relief. Phew.

Rusting Barbed Wire (2)

Rachel stands very still. She's visited this place before. She's recognising it. The familiarity is at once reassuring and deeply frightening. What had been a nightmare is now, by some dreadful self-fulfilling prophecy, very real. For what seems like aeons she stands gazing at Jack. He had made death look so easy. He had taken a breath, hung onto it a little longer, and then let go. Here, Rachel doesn't feel anything. Here, is a profoundly peaceful place filled with a love that requires no emotion to express it; a place akin to a tired mum gazing upon her newborn.

Then, she stepped forward, kissed him, and whispered, "I love you, Dad." And this action broke the spell. This action had the child in her crying out for help, had the child in her pressing the red resuscitation button . . .

Bells ringing. Sleepy night nurses leaping into action. Tired doctors entering through the curtains at a ferocious speed. All in some kind of weird choreography. And Rachel finds herself further and further away from her father. Everyone else is taking up the space, squeezing in-between. And then, "He's NFR." And, "I'm sorry." And a man in worn T-shirt and jeans is removing a stethoscope from his ears.

"What?"

"Not for resuscitation. I'm sorry."

Rachel runs, runs for her life, out of the ward, through the half-lit corridor, and further on into darker places.

In the distance there is a dim light and she heads for this, crashing through some double doors and into a small chapel. She paces up and down. Jesus is nailed to a cross on the wall, painted blood dripping from his feet, his mournful eyes gazing at her. She strides to and fro like a caged tiger with no way to escape. Then seeing a fine porcelain statue of Jesus she marches straight over to it and, in one punchy movement, pushes against it with the flat of her hands. Jesus rocks on the plinth. He has a benign smile on his face. His hands are outstretched in a gesture of greeting. Then he topples and smashes into tiny shards against the hard floor. Rachel is at once on her knees grappling to put him together again, her palms bleeding from a cut. And then, she is bayoneted in her side by a memory . . .

She is sixteen years old. Rebecca (eight) is standing in front of her, taunting her. "I'm telling Dad and you won't sit down for a week. You know you can't be trusted."

It's raining. Rebecca's long black hair is streaking across her face. She's laughing. And she's breathless. From the running in the rain and the laughing . . . There's the sound of thunder and the sparks of lightening. Rachel steps towards Rebecca and pushes her hard in the chest, and Rebecca steps backwards, slipping on some mud but still laughing. She grabs the rusting barbed wire but it doesn't hold her, and her face registers the full horror before the wire snaps, and then another wire, and then another, and the fence breaks like a weeping violin. Rebecca falls backwards into the mineshaft.

Rachel's hands, impotently reaching outwards to save Rebecca, flail in the darkness.

That Dreadful Day (2)

Sixteen-year-old Rachel slips stealthily around the side of the house. As she bends beneath the kitchen window she closes her eyes and holds her breath. Two sure-footed steps and she is clear of being caught. One. Two.

She reaches into her pocket and pulls out a potato knife. The blade slides easily between her bedroom window frames. She slides the catch open. The chipped blue paint is testimony to the number of times she has done this before.

Today she has never felt more in terror of being caught. She has never returned this late before. It's so dark. And how did it get this late?

Noiselessly the window slides up and Rachel is in.

She shuts the window behind her and crawls quickly under her blankets. She should have shed the damp clothes. And really should have removed her muddy shoes. They are tainting the fresh scented bed sheets.

Her flesh creeps with the cold from the ice generating in her stomach. Underneath the blankets she cannot get warm. That place between her legs is frozen.

The door swings open. And the light switched on. Her mother is standing, staring at her, into her.

How could Mum know?

And then her father is there too, standing behind her mother, with a stranger's face. A big man turned into a shadow, dark lines drawn across his sallow skin. He looks at her and then his features begin to dissolve; they fold and quiver. And Rachel cannot bear to look at him, whoever he is. He turns and leaves, carrying with him such heaviness that his spine hunches over under the weight.

Her mother sits on the edge of the bed, clearing her throat, finding her voice. Rachel is disgusted with herself. With what she has done. But something in her refuses to yield to her parents' distress.

How could they know?

How could they know about Alan?

Alan was twenty-one. He drove an E-Type Jag and dressed like David Bowie. The fifth-form's 'in crowd', whom Rachel only orbited like a distant planet, were mesmerised when he screeched to a halt outside the school gates. And when he leaned on the horn they watched, open-mouthed, as Rachel, Rachel Tangye, of all people, ran to the passenger door and hopped in. They drove off, Led Zepp's All Of My Love loudly providing the backing track to an unbelievable scene in the movie of Rachel's small life.

He parked close to where she lived and they left the car and walked through the tall ferns to a familiar clearing. He had one hand inside her school blouse and her heart was beating so fast she wondered if it would stop dead. By the time they lay on the ground there was such frenzied impatience that neither of them noticed Rebecca glaring down at them, wondering what on earth they were doing.

Rachel's virginity lay in a damp pool beneath her. And she felt let down. Endless hours of kissing, of hot wet tongues, had been much more exciting and brought greater pleasure than this forbidden fucking.

"Did you come?" he asked. But she didn't know what he meant. "Do you think your little sister wants some of the action?" Cocky now. Lighting a cigarette.

Rachel turns her head and sees Rebecca; glares at Rebecca. How dare she . . . "Get the hell home."

Rebecca laughs. "I'm telling mum." Then she turns tail and runs, swift on her feet, with a strength that belies her eight years. There's a freedom in that movement, an easiness that is almost spiritual. It's as if she'd learned from an animal, a horse.

"You can't catch me; I'm telling Dad," she taunts, laughter bubbling out of her like water from the mine.

"Just you wait girl!" But Rachel blushes, embarrassed to be caught being the child she still cleaves to.

Alan laughs and they have sex again.

It was only a hymen.

Then once more, before he lets go of her.

It was only a penis.

Rachel's mother finally speaks, sotto voce. "Rebecca is missing. She didn't come home from school. Your father found a scrap of her cardigan on some barbed wire."

They don't know. They don't know.

"The thing is Rachel, the barbed wire . . . the barbed wire . . . it was broken . . . and there may have been an accident. Your sister may be hurt."

They don't know. They don't know that I had sex.

"Rachel, are you listening to me? Do you understand what I'm saying? The mine rescue will search in the morning, as soon as it's light enough." Tears now.

"Stop! Stop! Don't tell me anything." Rachel covers her ears and closes her eyes.

The back door slams shut as Rachel's father leaves with a torch held tightly in his white knuckled hands. Ruth leaps up. "Look after your brothers." For a timeless moment Rachel and Ruth look at each other. Searching for truth. There is something telling in her mother's eyes. With closed mouth and silent tongue she is saying, "I am on to you, Rachel. I am on to you, my girl." It is so perceptible, so primal that Rachel casts her eyes down. But that look will stare out of every mirror that she ever summons the courage to gaze into.

Ruth grabs her coat and runs after Jack. Runs into the dark night after her last-born.

Life

A large crowd has gathered at the top of the mine-shaft. It is still raining and a biting wind burns the flesh drawn taught and translucent across their anxious faces.

The light from their torches is fading like their hopes in the grey dawn. Jack and Ruth hold onto each other tight, as if at any moment one or other of them might plummet into the abyss.

The mine rescue team work quietly, reverentially, without a trace of suppressed optimism. They know. They know that if the little girl has fallen into this shaft than she is dead. No-one could survive the fall intact. She will be black and blue with abstract streaks of red from her ricocheting descent. And her eyes will have popped out of her head.

There are no miracles to be found at the bottom of a mine. There is only the light in the heart of the man who lifts the small girl into his arms and pulls twice on the rope that supports him.

As they ascend towards the light he tries, vainly, to clean her up, but there is too much tin-red slurry. It is all too much. But he looks into her mouth because he needs to know . . . He looks into her mouth and sees that it is clean. She died before she hit the bottom. All he can do now is hold her.

Rachel, sleep-walking, stands in the distance, away from the crowd, where from her dream-world she watches a nightmare unfold.

The mine rescue man holding onto the broken Rebecca has to look at her waiting parents, while he, suspended in the air, is powerless. He will take this day to his grave and only there will this memory rest.

As they are lowered down, Ruth rushes forward, slipping in the mud. Jack follows, slipping too, until they are both on their knees, cradling their daughter.

"This is not my Rebecca . . . Is not my Rebecca . . . Not my Rebecca . . . My Rebecca. Rebecca . . . My baby Rebecca." Ruth rocks her child, trying to put her back together again. And Jack, who has managed until now to hold himself together, lets out such a primordial cry it washes through the hearts of every man present, reverberating into all of their futures.

Rachel must return now to the safety of her bed, to the safety of her lie, her safe black lie. So she slips away, unnoticed, back into the illusion known as reality, back into the illusion known as amnesia.

And so it is that a dark dismal day becomes the dawning of the decomposition of Jack and Ruth, written as an unfathomable lament in the repertoire of their loving lives.

Several Drinks For Jack

Harry and Mark are sitting in the kitchen. Jack's bottle of Glenfiddich on the table and two glasses half-filled with the malt ceremoniously in front of each of them. They lift their glasses. "To Jack." There is a chink and they knock back the shots in one.

"Your father would be mad as hell thinking he'd left this behind – have another."

Mark doesn't protest. Although he loves Harry like an uncle, he'd give anything to be doing this with his father.

"You know Ruth was the one who always thought Jack would be the death of her. I must admit I thought the old bugger would outlive us all. Never in a million did I see myself living past him. Don't know I will."

They sit in silence, each trying to absorb the sadness that was creeping up from their toes like gangrene.

Harry looks around the kitchen, examining all the spaces that Jack took up.

"I remember the day you moved in here like it was yesterday. Your father nearly set fire to the place trying to get that thing lighted." He points at the Aga.

Mark laughs. "You know for years I thought everyone lit their stoves with a bloody great gas bottle."

Harry grows silent and laughs again.

Harry's laughter makes Mark smile.

"What?"

"Oh it's nothing."

"Go on, tell me." Mark refills their glasses.

"Don't suppose you remember the day you came here."

"No, not really. I must have been three, three at the most."

"Your father did that apple core trick of his."

"Oh! Yeah. Jees that's great. I've seen him do that many times."

"Well two days later I have to borrow Jack's car and take all you kids to the infirmary – he's refereeing a rugby match. Ruth was jumping mad. I'll never forget it. I sat in the car, outside the casualty department, with you and Becky. I was scared stiff in case Becky woke up. I was never any good with babies. Then I saw Ruth with John, Matthew and Rachel all trooping behind her, proudly holding up their bandaged thumbs. I thought I'd die laughing.

"And when your Da' came home from the club he was that proud of them. He was as drunk as can be and Ruth had a devil of a job stopping him from waking them up. He just wanted to pat them on the back . . . He made them breakfast the next day – pancakes. We all had pancakes.

"You won't believe how many times I've tried to do that trick. Dad used to say it was easy, that it was all in your head, but I couldn't get past the idea that it was gonna hurt.

"That was your father all over; he never let fear stop him doing anything. Can't tell you how many bruises I got believing that 'all in your head' line of his."

The door opens and Matthew comes in.

"Thought I might find you two here. Have you seen Rachel? She's not answering her phone." Matthew looks at the scene. "It's seven thirty in the morning."

"Have a drink boy. Rachel will come round when she's ready; she's always bottled things up, always slipped away like a wounded animal." Harry removes the cap from the bottle.

Matthew fetches himself a glass. "You know I can't stand this stuff but he would expect it, wouldn't he?" He raises his glass. "Cheers Dad." He knocks the drink back and then grimaces, as if he'd just taken medicine. "The hospital said Rachel left around six. Suppose she's asleep. Must have been a rough night. How's Mum?"

"Pretending to be asleep. Maybe that's what Rachel's doing too. Here, have another drink. We can't let the old man down." Mark pours them all another.

That Dreadful Day (3)

Ruth is curled into a ball in the middle of the double bed. She left Mark and Harry to it – couldn't stand to have anyone around her. She wanted Jack. Couldn't cope with the idea of his body left alone in a cold place, a cold hospital . . .

...They tried to take Rebecca away from me. I was holding the little mite so tight and the policeman was saying something about a post-mortem and I was sobbing and saying, "No, you can't have her like this; you can't have her like this." Only Jack understood. He took our little Becky from my arms and he looked at the two policemen walking towards us to take her away and he stood up and said, "We're taking our daughter home, and that's an end to it." He said it with such force, such dignity, although his heart was breaking. Then two firemen caught the policeman by the arms and they didn't say anything, but they nodded at Jack and he nodded too. He didn't need the firemen's help, he would have killed those policeman rather than let them take her just then.

When the babies were really tiny it was Jack who bathed them. I couldn't. I was so afraid that they'd break. But they were safe as could be in his great big hands.

So we brought Rebecca's broken little body back home. She was covered in mud, red sticky mud, through her hair, everywhere. We bathed her together, changing the water three times, each time watching the filthy water circle down the plughole. And I could see her dropping down that shaft, spinning like the water, and I was thinking: Why didn't God take me? Why didn't God take me? Her little face... Her beautiful little face, all torn up . . . We dressed her in her Sunday School clothes. I knew as I was doing it that she'd prefer trousers; she was such a tomboy. Jack wrapped her in a blanket and he sat in the chair next to the Aga holding her; he wasn't going to let them take her away until her hair was dry. The policemen waited outside. They've capped the old shafts now. Oh Jack . . .

Several More Drinks For Jack

Harry moves his glass, very deliberately just out of his reach. Then he folds his arms and leans forward. Seeing this sudden seriousness come over him, Mark and Matthew put their glasses down and also lean forward. "I'm gonna tell you something about your father . . . " Harry pauses for dramatic effect. Mark and Matthew are rapt. "He couldn't fucking fish." Harry leans back in his chair and takes his drink.

Mark and Matthew look at each other in disbelief; first shocked that Harry had said fucking, and then bewildered because didn't Jack always come back from fishing trips with more mackerel than Ruth knew what to do with? They both laugh and Harry continues. "Those fingers of his were like sausages; he couldn't tie the hooks on."

"Harry! You said fucking," Mark says, still incredulous.

"Learned that from your dad. I'll tell you another thing about him: he used to go about with a business card in his top pocket, silver-edged it were, and written in the middle of it, in that fancy script you get, was 'fuck off'. He was a one-off right enough, a man with style."

"I've Killed Jesus"

Rachel comes to. A man in jeans and T-shirt is shaking
her shoulder. She wakes like someone coming out of a
long hibernation. She's stiff and her hands are sore. She
registers the cuts in her hands, and then gets a vivid
picture of Rebecca grasping barbed wire. She takes in
the porcelain shards, the bits of Jesus, her dead father
and murdered sister, and she looks up at the man above
her. "I've killed . . . Jesus . . . I've killed . . . "

Thinking she is just trying to apologise for the breaking of the statue he says, "Don't worry, he'll forgive you."

Rachel looks at him, deeply serious. "Are you sure?"

"Of course. Come on, let's get you up. You must
have fainted and knocked it over. You've had a shock.

We'll go back to the ward and I'll look at these cuts. The nurse has phoned your brother Matthew and he's going to break the news to your mother. Now, is there someone who can come and collect you?"

Rachel starts to shake, shake with the terrible cold that circles her body like an easterly wind."My father is dead."

"Yes, he is. It was very quick; he would not have suffered very much."

Not have suffered very much. Rachel repeats this phrase over and over in her head as the man dresses her wounds. It dawns: he was the one with the stethoscope. I'm sorry, he'd said, when her father had just died. And she'd watched him die. She'd watched his last breath fill up his cheeks and then slowly leave his lips like he was blowing out smoke. He gave up smoking. He said he got a sharp chest pain as he crossed the field to walk back to work one day, so he reached his hand into his top pocket and threw his cigarettes and lighter across the field. What did her Dad say?

The doctor finishes looking at Rachel's hands."Only scratches; I can't see any splinters."Rachel looks at his name badge: Gwyn. Dr. Gwyn Pritchard. She can't bear to look him in the eyes, not after what she has done. How could she have harmed Rebecca? How could she have killed love?

Ponytail nurse comes into the clinical room. "Would

you like to see your father now?"

"What?"

"You can sit with your father now, if you'd like. You don't have to. Whatever you wish. I'll get you some tea."

Rachel stands up and walks slowly through the ward. The man opposite her father's bed is moaning about the noise and how it is keeping him awake. She pulls back the curtains and gasps: Jack is lying flat; he's been washed; his head is on one pillow; and his hair has been combed. A stranger has been kind to his poor dead body. And yet it is plain for Rachel to see that Jack is not there. That Jack Tangye has left the building. The essence of Jack drifted away with his last breath. Nevertheless, she sits next to him; she's in a state of shock. She is utterly cognizant of the day's discoveries and events. She could list them in order: Abigail died on an empty grave; Johnny Daylight didn't die and may even be alive still; she slammed the phone down on her mother; her mother has probably got dementia; her father is dead; and she killed her sister. Rachel digs into the scratches on her hands until they bleed. But she cannot feel anything. What did you say Dad?

Ponytail nurse, Trevor, comes through the curtains and gives Rachel a cup of tea.

"My father said something to me before he died. He said something and I can't remember what it was."

Nurse Trevor taps the side of his own head. "Don't

worry, it's in there somewhere. It'll come back to you; important things always do." Trevor looks at Jack. "He was a real gent."

"I think I'll go now." Rachel stands up, gives the tea back, and like a spectral angel quietly leaves.

Outside, the calm that comes after a storm reveals a night sky filled with twinkling dots and the band of light of the Milky Way clearly visible. And if only Rachel would look up from the ground, she would see a shooting star streaming across the heavens.

Inside, two porters come and collect Jack's body. They lift him into a metal box, which is supported on legs which run on wheels and they cover this with a sheet and place a thin pillow at one end, so now it looks as though they are pushing an empty trolley. Jack would appreciate this deceptive act. He would, if he could, buy them a drink.

When Rachel arrives home, a journey she cannot recall, she closes her curtains and unplugs her phone. She goes to her desk and removes the duffle bag which contains Abigail's letters. She sits down, takes a pen and a piece of writing paper and begins to write . . .

Dear Abigail,
    Now I am you we are even . . .

Four

Dislocation

Rachel is sitting at her desk in the small living room. The curtains are drawn and the only illumination is a suffused shaft of light that creeps in around the partially open door leading from the hallway.

She is hunched over and writing . . .

Dear Abigail,

Dislocation is not so difficult to understand. I was once a sperm, and once an ovum, both bits of me in brooding expectation, anticipating the moment, the miracle, the fuck, the Mum, the Dad, the me, the Rachel in me . . .

She scrunches the paper into a small ball as she

tries to make sense of who she is now. She has been ill-conceived. Living a life believing that Rebecca died in some tragic accident, when all the time the truth was eating her up inside and some fearful will in her would not allow it to surface, not allow her to own it. Now in the dark shadow of Jack's death the truth is an avenging angel and what rocks her to and fro in her seat is not self-pity – for the truth has severed the chains that have long been holding her – but rather the knowledge that she must atone, must make amends. How can she ask Rebecca for forgiveness? How can she ask Jack?

An eye for an eye, isn't that what the Bible says?

Ruth(1)

Ruth opens her eyes and shuts them again. Jack died yesterday. Her husband died yesterday. She struggles to sit up, pushing against the hard facts of death. Then she smells him, a sweet, rancid smell of stale alcohol. This used to repulse her, but now she follows it, follows it like a dog borne away on a scent. And for a moment his death is simply a nightmare and she rebukes herself for such ludicrous confusion. But then hadn't she been doing lots of stupid things lately? Hadn't Jack told her she needed to concentrate more . . . ? On what? The job in hand. That's what he'd wanted her to do: concentrate on the job in hand.

She finds herself in the living room, gazing down at Harry who is stretched out on the sofa, covered with an old blanket. Matthew is on the other sofa, curled up on his side, his hands cradling his head, as if, even in sleep, he is hungover. Jack died yesterday. My dear sweet Jack died yesterday. Ruth walks to the kitchen, where two empty bottles of Glenfiddich stand, discarded, on the table top. She looks at the three empty glasses and the sweet sticky rings where they have marked the wood, all ghosts from yesterday. How could they? How could they drink his drink? Ruth sits down, angry for being angry. He'd always been a drinker: would come home from the rugby club happy as could be, smiling at her, knowing he was in trouble and somehow charming his way around her so the very next weekend she would be digging in her purse, looking for some money so he could go out and enjoy himself again.

Rebecca's death changed all of that. Not one drink passed his lips, from that day to this that made him happy.

That Dreadful Day (4)

Ruth remembers Jack sitting on the edge of Rachel's bed. He was telling her, as he had the boys, that Rebecca had died in our arms. We'd agreed it was the best way – the best way to keep the other children safe.

Then I look at Rachel's shoes, covered in mud they were. I look at our daughter's face and she, the child, the poor sweet child, is obviously distressed, is taking in the information as if she has just heard it for the first time. But there is something else, some incomprehensible other, that I know to be there, as only a mother can. Here in the weft of one lie is the warp of another, making the thin fabric that will barely bind our family together. I had to hold on; I dug my fists into the wool of Jack's pullover and grabbed it with all my might as the idea that Rachel might have had something to do with Rebecca's death, bangs like a rock, loudly, against my head. Then I pray, like I've never prayed before. Jack must not see this. Please God do not let Jack see this. Rachel leapt out of bed and there is mud staining her clean white sheets and I gasp and mercifully Jack turns, in that moment of saving grace, Jack turns, and in that is saved, saved from some knowledge that might have killed him.

Didn't we all die a little that day? Didn't we all fall down that shaft after Rebecca? And, as it turned out, no one more than Rachel. Has she not been dead in her heart since that very day? My daughters, my darling daughters. My husband, my darling husband . . .

Rachel's Wish Come True (2)

Rachel is running along the lane, pushing the push-chair deliberately over the rough stones so that Rebecca is bounced up and down. Rebecca is laughing. Laughing and shouting out, "Weeeeeeeeeeee!" as she careers through dried up puddles. And then they reach a small incline, and Rachel is able to let go of the pushchair, race ahead of it and catch Rebecca coming towards her, independently, blindly trusting the procession of her life. Rachel's arms stretch out in greeting and she catches her little sister and, for a moment, all is still and quiet, as the two take easy breaths between their laughter, and just here, in this silent grace, Rachel feels love. It catches in her heart and moves slowly outwards, expanding into her entire being, a glowing warmth that is both ephemeral and solid; something that she can give back to the world. Rebecca lifts her soft baby arms upwards and spontaneously hugs her older sister. Caught in the sunbeam of an ordinary moment, in an ordinary day, in an ordinary lane, between ordinary children, something extraordinary happens.

Dear Abigail,
   Why didn't you let me drown?
Rachel

The Cavalry

There is a loud, persistent knocking at the door. "Rachel. We know you're in there. Come on, let us in."

Rachel looks up from her desk through the gloom of her life to the door. She has to tell herself what to do: stand up; walk to the door; open the door; let them in. She can hear herself, she can hear all the words, but they are strung together on the other side . . . the other side of herself. She gazes at the letter and crumples it up, and then she inspects the small cuts in her hands and tears roll down her cheeks in huge splashing drops. Jack is dead. Her father is dead.

"Rachel, if you don't let us in we'll take the door down." Matthew, more persistent.

Mark says, "Brilliant idea mate, get your tool kit."

Matthew turns to his younger brother. "What would I do with the tool kit? Remove the door handle? The bolt would still be bolted. Idiot."

"Rach! Rach! Open the door! Matthew is beating me."

Rachel stands up, walks to the door, opens the door, and lets them in.

"Jees sis, we've been worried sick about you. And you need a bit of light in here." Mark grabs the curtain.

"No! Don't! Leave it! Please leave it! I have such a headache."

Matthew takes his time, looking about him, adjusting to the darkness. He remembers how long it was before Rachel finally came out of her dark room following Rebecca's accident. He remembers how silent she was, and how when she did speak it was in a tiny voice, a voice as soft as Abigail's. A shiver runs through him. "Mum needs you Rachel. Whatever you may be thinking or feeling, Mum needs you. We all do. Harry is a mess."

"Come on sis – we've got a new fridge," Mark adds. Mark, bless him.

All three of them are in acute pain now. This is how grief works; it catches you on its sharp point, spins you around, until, before you know it, you are twisted, helplessly twisted, on its blade.

Rachel's First Funeral

In the photograph, Rebecca is holding Mr. Pegotty, her rooster. He was some rooster, a real strutter: combed top hat, double-breasted jacket, and feathered tails. He stalked his hen harem on drumstick legs. "A cock with an enormous doodle do," Jack would say, and then laugh the loudest.

"Rachel, it's time."

Rachel turns to see Matthew standing in his black suit. He's holding the kitchen door open, waiting for her. She places the photograph back alongside the others and follows Matthew outside, where seeing the hearse with Jack's coffin in it, she stops again. It shocks her. She hadn't anticipated the coffin, hadn't prepared herself. She climbs into the black limousine and sits next to Ruth, who immediately takes her hand. Rachel searches her memory for Rebecca's funeral and all she can find is a view of herself being left behind: a small child standing on a threshold of a place where she dare not go. Although she would not have been a small child, she would have been sixteen.

Matthew, Harry, Mark, Matthew's wife Lucy, Sam and Jade are all utterly devoid of colour. Jack left them and he took with him a rainbow. None of them are fully present; they are black and white facsimiles paying their last respects, their dignified farewells. They are fugitives seeking refuge in their lesser selves: the part of them not quite ready to deal with the truth; the part of them that must learn to accept; the part of them prepared to spend a lifetime in the process.

Carn Brea village chapel is full to capacity. All the seats are taken and people are standing down the side walls and gathered at the back. Men mostly, bursting out of their suits or lost in them. Men from the rugby clubs, the British Legion, ex-miners, ex-airforce, drinkers from the pubs, landlords and landladies, rich and poor – just people who loved Jack.

When the hymns begin, it sounds like a male voice choir. "How great thou art ... How great thou art ... "And somewhere in the harmonies there is enormous comfort.

It's the first Monday of the year and, befitting the mood, the heavens have opened. The rain is torrential.

The Tangye family slot back into their Sunday School positions, taking up the first two pews. Jack's coffin at the front sits miserably underneath the weight of a wild and extravagant arrangement of white lilies, which bedeck its shiny surface. Evergreen leaves trail down the side through the brass handles.

"How great thou art . . . "

Sympathy and sorrow pour into the hymns, and then Harry is invited forward to read the eulogy he never prepared for.

"Jack Tangye was my one true friend . . . He is . . . He was . . . the only man I have ever met who wasn't afraid to love. And he loved everything. But nothing more than his family."

Harry looks at the diminished family and directly at Ruth, who cannot hold back her tears, and Harry's own suddenly begin to fall. Not alone in the quiet of his garden, but here, publicly, for all to see, and he takes his time to mentally apologise to his dearest friend, before bravely continuing. "I can't remember how many times I had to hold the old bugger's coat . . . but I'm telling you this, without Jack I would not have had a life. Not a life worth living." Pushing back through the embarrassed laughter and tears, Harry returns to his seat. He did his best. If Jack were able he'd buy him a drink, and this thought carries Harry to the cemetery where he, Matthew and Mark assist the undertaker to carry the coffin.

"I guess this is the last time we have to carry Dad," Mark says, and Matthew laughs and Harry laughs and the ripple of light even in the darkest black soon has them, all three, holding court at the funeral tea.

Ruth sits on the sofa with Sam and Jade cuddled up close. Lucy, balancing a plate on her knee filled with food she can't eat, sits on the arm of the sofa, and Rachel stands behind them all, leaning up against the Aga, trying to find warmth. People they hardly know stand around their glasses charged in the name of Jack.

Harry, recovered, and now cast into the limelight as chief storyteller of Jack anecdotes, is suddenly, if momentarily, happy in his new role in life . . .

"And I'm telling you, without a word of a lie, he grabbed the hatchet and split the cockpit in two! He dragged Ernie out – and you all know how big Ernie was – right across the runway. Well a minute hadn't passed before the whole blessed thing went up in smoke . . . and you know what he said? He said that he 'couldn't let Ernie burn, because he needed him for the match', and Ernie is still lying there on the ground wondering why he's still alive and the ambulances are careering across the airfield and then he said, 'Shall we all have a pint boys?' He gave that big smile of his and we all walked away, like nothing at all had happened." Harry falls silent, closes his eyes, and watches their airforce days in front of him. And a smile creeps across his face until he is almost smug, and this infects everyone.

All, that is, exept Rachel, who slides open the sideboard drawer and removes Rebecca's wooden box. She puts on her winter coat and nobody notices her leave.

What About Them Apples?

Matthew, Mark and Harry have taken their jackets off and have their shirt sleeves rolled up. They each have drunk-red faces and perspiration blisters on their foreheads. Ruth is on the edge of her seat, leaning forward, intent.

Mark says, "Okay, on three. One. Two. Three."

They each raise an apple above their heads and smash it down onto their upturned thumbs. They all succeed. Three cores pop out onto the table top. Yells of delight fill the air. Then there is a deep silence laden with an If only Jack were alive to see this.

Ruth sits back in her chair. Relieved. Jack would be proud, proud as could be. But she looks at her two sons and she knows in the heart of this small victory that they are biting their lips, stanching their tears.

They have, and John too, spent their lives living up to Jack, trying to please him, trying to be like him, a man's man. Ruth watches as they fill their glasses . . . If they but knew that Jack loved them, loved them all the time, whether they were beaten on the rugby field or not. He couldn't show them, that's all. Not like he could his girls. Silly man. Silly overprotective man. Ruth wipes the small tear from the corner of her eye, and in a moment of sweet clarity she wonders if her sons will find their own strength now – now that they don't have Jack's? Are they free? Free to be themselves . . . ?

Hell's Mouth (1)

Rachel has walked the four miles to Hell's Mouth, clutching the wooden box under her arm. She now sits on the cliff top staring down at the sea as it churns over and around the rocks. The tide is out and it has stopped raining, although the sky remains a muted grey.

Rachel can't feel anything. She is resting in the sump at the bottom of the shaft where she is totally supported. Nothing matters here. She could stay here indefinitely. On the way down, she hit the sharp girders, which stuck out from the walls. She banged up against the granite boulders and she closed her eyes to the rusting chains that clanked against the wooden pit props, which in fathoms marked her descent. Why would she begin to climb up? When in climbing she would have to face these things once again and somehow get past them.

She stands, a remote viewer, and watches as Rachel leaps off the cliff. Watches her coat gets caught in the breeze and, for a moment, be held in the air, before it separates from her to be blown in a gust back onto the cliff top – something of the moment saved by its very lightness.

A dog walker, an innocent bystander, observes the woman, the coat, the wooden box. The woman on the rocks. None of it can be real. A policeman arrives. A policeman who is afraid of heights has to lean over the cliff edge and talk on his radio. A coastguard lashes his Land Rover to the cliff top and abseils over the edge. The St. Ives inshore and offshore lifeboats. Lifeboats. Come to the rescue. Rescue. Then a noisy helicopter, from Culdrose, suspends a man on an umbilical cord while the rotary blades ape the sound of a foetal heartbeat. He reaches the woman. The poor dead woman. Smashed hard against the rocks. She is taken in a lifeboat to the place of the dead and dearly departed. How could she? How could Jack Tangye's daughter do this?

And of course Jack's daughter cannot do this. She has not got the courage. She can imagine it, she can visualise all these heroic men trying to save her – for isn't that what she is used to? Yes, Rachel can wish these things . . . but there is no escaping or hiding from the truth.

She picks up the small, wooden box and walks along the road, her head bent, praying for destiny's assistance. Wondering if, in the turmoil of her mind, she really did hear Jack shouting at her at all. "If it takes off, we'll know it's not dead."

She is not Abigail. She is not Abigail. She is not Abigail. She is Rachel Tangye . . . Whatever that means.

Rachel Tangye: A Work In Progress

"I am Rachel Tangye and I murdered my sister. My sister Rebecca."

The policeman, suddenly interested, looks at the slightly built woman standing before the front desk and puts down his crossword puzzle. Underneath her dishevelled appearance is a calmness that has him worried.

"Okay, so you have my attention." It is the first Monday of the year and he suddenly feels exhilarated. He takes down some details and then takes Rachel to a small room. It has a desk and three plastic chairs in it. She sits and lifts out all the memorabilia from the wooden box and lays it carefully on the table. She folds her hands in her lap and patiently waits.

The policeman and a detective are observing her, on a television screen, in an adjacent room.

"Claims she murdered her sister – pushed her down a mineshaft."

"Shafted her sister. That's novel! See what you can find out. I'll have a word."

The detective looks at the report sheet, puts his 'jolly' head on, and steps into the room. "Hello." He consults the report sheet. "Miss Tangye. Shall I call you Rachel?"

Rachel nods.

"I see you're a receptionist at the Headland Hotel . . . Laid off for the winter . . . "

Rachel nods.

"Married, no children."

"No. Not married. Yes. No children."

The detective brings his chair around so he is sitting next to Rachel but facing her. Rachel has time to think of the hard chairs she'd seen in films.

"My colleague has just gone to check the records, but perhaps you'd like to tell me what you told him."

"I pushed my sister down a mineshaft. Here." She passes him the death certificate and the newspaper reports. Which he carefully reads.

"These all appear to say that it was an accident. An accident that happened . . . What . . . ? Over thirty years ago?"

Rachel nods.

"Why wait 'til now?"

"I've only just remembered. Something happened. Something bad happened . . . "

"Go on."

"My father died. It was his funeral today. He died last week and I don't know how but somehow . . . the shock . . . yes, the shock . . . brought back this memory. I pushed her. I was angry and pushed her. She fell back against the barbed wire. The wire broke. I tried to stop her. I reached forward but slipped in the mud and couldn't grab her. I sat on the edge waiting for her to climb back up. I sat there for hours until I shook with the cold. She didn't climb up."

The detective reaches into his pocket and passes Rachel a clean, pressed and neatly folded handkerchief. He waits, some while, until she is recovered.

"Forgive me, but what makes you so sure that this memory is more real than the truth you have lived with for all these years?"

"The knot I've carried in my stomach, since that day, has unravelled." She looks up at him with such ironic inno-cence that he cannot doubt her.

"What about other members of your family?"

"They think Rebecca's death was an accident. Can you imagine if they knew? Can you imagine how much for-giveness that would require?"

As Rachel spoke the words she heard clanging cymbals in her head, her father's last words: Rachel forgive . . . Becky . . . The look her mother would give her, those Granny

Opie eyes blinking away the truth: changing from stony hatred to soft belly love in a second. Real love. Real unconditional love.

Rachel begins to sob, loudly. "I didn't mean it. I didn't mean it. I loved Rebecca. I loved her like she was my own child. My very best friend."

"If you didn't intend to kill your sister then it is still an accident."

"What do you think?"

"I think the mining company should have maintained the fence. That's what I think. Excuse me a moment – I'll get you a cup of tea."

The detective leaves. Rachel is recalling small moments that now make sense, small intuitions that she could never put her finger on. Her parents knew: they've known all along. They've each sat on the edge, waiting for her epiphany, waiting to catch her as she fell into the truth.

Outside the interview room the detective is wondering what to do with the woman. Then his mate, Adrian, a solicitor, walks down the corridor that leads away from the cells.

"Just the man."

"What?"

"Small favour. It's nothing."

"You still owe me from the last small favour! In fact a shed load of small favours."

The detective explains the situation while Adrian thinks,

dreamily, about having a cigarette. A post-coital cigarette. Now that would be splendid.

"Sounds like she needs a confessional not an interview room."

"Go on, it won't take you five minutes."

"But I'm a solicitor."

"You'd make a better priest."

"Cunt!" Adrian steps into the interview room where Rachel is very subdued. He picks up the photographs of Rebecca, the small picture Bible, the newspaper cuttings and the death certificate and puts everything back into the box, closing the lid. "CID will carry out a full investigation but as far as I can tell there is no case to answer."

Rachel stares back at him. She'd hoped for life imprisonment. Or the electric chair. Some way to atone. Adrian continues, "Somehow you must find the grace to accept what happened. There is power in acceptance, you know?"

"I can't explain. I just need to surrender to something. To give myself up."

"Perhaps you just need to forgive. The world turns on 'what ifs': What if I'd stayed home? What if I'd not stayed home? What if I'd smiled instead of shouted? We're all of us irresponsible fuckwits . . . And there it is." Adrian leaves.

The detective returns with a cup of hot tea, which Rachel gratefully accepts.

"I'm exhausted," she says, and the detective nods.

Salient Plot Point

When Rachel arrives back at the bungalow there are only a few people left. She slips into the kitchen and returns the wooden box to the sideboard drawer, burying it beneath letters, bills and the junk mail that choke up people's lives. She finds Ruth in the living room with the others, Harry still talking . . .

"You're absolutely correct. Jack did reach in his pocket and throw his cigarettes and lighter across the field, but here's the bit he didn't tell you . . . The very next day he had every man from the machine shop scouring that field until they were found . . . "

Rachel squeezes in next to Ruth and puts her arm around her mother. They look at each other a long time, taking stock, assessing. Rachel wants to blurt it all out. To tell her mother that she knows, she knows, and is so deeply sorry. And so grateful – for loving her anyway.

But the ice packed around her is too hard and the thaw must happen slowly, so, for now, she holds Ruth's hand tight and in her heart she blesses her tired parents and she wrestles with an important truth. She is loved.

Five

So There Is A Future

Dear Abigail,

I cried when mum first fell from her pedestal, shattered pieces of precious porcelain, insides spilling, willing imperfections. I felt a kind of shame when father did the same, a drowning man lying in a drunken stupor, weak and human, not 'super' at all. Gluing the pieces back together, I realise, too late, that I created their fall by building the damned pedestal . . .

Rachel xx

PS. Thank you for saving me.

Big Brother

Rachel sits on a bench on Platform Two of Redruth Railway Station, mentally writing her letters to Abigail. The last time she was here it was to say goodbye to Mark after Jack's funeral. That was four years ago, but might as well have been yesterday.

Now she waits for John, who has travelled across the world to say goodbye to their mother before her brain eats away her memories of him.

He arrives in autumn, under a blue sky, his hair prematurely white and his belly big and soft, in a Jack Tangye kind of way.

They are strangers really, neither knowing anything about the other's life. But there is between them a deep understanding that exists in their blood, a genetic Velcro that binds them.

Ruth did not survive Jack's death. Most of her had simply tried to follow him, and what was left was an exquisite shell, that which you might find washed up on the sands of a beach one day: pearly smooth interior; gnarled exterior. A fragile thing. An exquisite, fragile thing.

It seemed as though her insidious falling apart crept through her being and reached out, like deep roots searching for nourishment, trying to cling on but finding nothing there because the very ground around her began to shake, as, at first, small craters opened up in the earth, beginning in the adjacent field and growing ever closer, until part of the garage was sucked underground.

Subsidence, that's what they call it, when the ground gives way underneath you. Dementia is its name when it happens in your brain.

What remained of the bungalow after the ground swallowed its share was taken by thieves, who stole the lead, the copper pipes, the slate tiles, the granite lintels, the bath and the Aga.

Eventually a bulldozer flattened the area, and now, where once an ordinary family lived, rusting metal and brambles share the space. In the summer, dog-roses, wild orchids and foxgloves splash their colours everywhere and birds sing.

Ruth (2)

Ruth sits in the armchair next to her bed. The room is small and cozy. It has a large window which looks down over an enormous garden. Her glass cabinet is filled with ornaments and the walls are covered in family photographs. There is always a vase filled with flowers from Harry's garden. He walks the two miles every day to see her. It is his purpose, his promise to his friend.

Rachel walks in and gives her mum a kiss.

"Jack died yesterday. Your father died yesterday."

"No Mum. Dad died four years ago, almost five. It's 2004 now. I've got a surprise for you." John walks slowly around the corner. He'd strolled up the corridor, trying to psyche himself up, but he'd wandered into the day lounge and it had frightened him to see these people, so many confused and distressed, trying to make sense of what was the simple drinking of tea.

John turned and headed back towards room forty-one. He hovered for a few moments at the doorway, sneaking a look at his mother who had aged so much. Then her bright eyes caught him and she said, "Hello darling." She put out her arms and they hugged each other a long time. She knew him. She still knew him. That's all he wanted. To be recognised. Tears pricked their eyes and Rachel retreated from the pain of too much tenderness. "I'll come back for you," she said.

"OK dear," Ruth responded. And then to John, in explanation, "That's Rachel. She's my daughter."

"I know Mum," he said, clearing his throat. He stands up and stretches, as if he's just done something physically strenuous, and then looks out of the window, into the garden, gazing at a small fallen tree. It must have come down in a storm, he thinks; its branches are splayed across the lawn and some of its roots are still buried in the ground. Others hang impotently in the air. "Nice place, mum. This is a nice place." Tears threaten to fill his eyes.

Rachel sits in the art room, leafing through the portfolios that are the work of the residents. Art is part of their therapy. The work is primitive: amorphous shapes and bold primary colours. Ruth has done three drawings, all pencil sketches coloured in with crayon. Bright greens and yellows slide over pencilled edges into other shapes, into other colours. But it is possible to pick out identifiable things: a cat; a fairy with yellow wings; a face. Each page has blobs of red over it, like small bleeding wounds. Ruth still manages to write her name, and 'Ruth Tangye' is printed in thick black felt tip at the bottom right hand corner of each curled-up page.

On the wall hangs a spectacular painting in oils. It is a mixture of abstract and figurative work, and the colours are so beautifully combined that Rachel takes a long time to see it all. To the right is an image of a man: his head and naked torso. He is very lean, and his head is tilted back, and his eyes are closed. He is pale blue, which darkens to indigo at the edges. He has red lines coming away from his body so he is attached to something, or, in another moment, it looks as though these lines are piercing him. Attached? Or attacked? It is hard to tell. In the abstract world, which surrounds him there, is a wolf, a guardian, who stands at his right shoulder watching over him.

The signature reads 'Glen Mortensen-Cave'.

Healing Jesus

After visiting Ruth, John and Rachel drive to South Crofty. They are given a yellow hard hat and permission to look around. First they pass the field, empty of water now, its concrete lining fully exposed and revealing the truth to a long ago unanswered question.

Just behind the Robinson shaft headgear the pathway which was once the shortcut to their home is still clear and they follow it, knowing that at any minute they will come up against the mineshaft that Rebecca plunged down. It now has girders stretched across the mouth and a thick chain cage covers the top. It's not possible to see down through the girders because they are too tightly

254

packed.

"Wouldn't lose a match down through there," says John.

"No," Rachel replies, deciding to tell him, to tell him what happened. But not here. And not yet.

They walk on towards where the bungalow should be. Stumbling over the rubble and trying to find something familiar. John finds a stick, painted blue.

"Look! I bet this was part of the garage door."

Rachel looks sceptical.

"It was this colour. Don't you remember?" John breaks the wood into small sticks and hands one to Rachel. "Here, a small memento."

For a while they wonder off separately, kicking over their past. Then they come back together again and sit on a piece of abandoned mine equipment, neither of them knowing what it is.

"Mum didn't seem too bad."

"Yes, she was pleased to see you, she knew you."

"I was relieved. I can tell you. Tough shit isn't it? Tragic."

"It's very hard. Sometimes in-between visits I just forget. I somehow slip back to when she was normal. So when I visit again it's like reliving it from the beginning, from the first hospital days . . . "

This idea knocks between them like a ball in a

pinball machine. They take time to listen to the bird song. To look around. To observe the space their home took up. The space between them.

"How you doing otherwise? How's work?"

"I'm laid off for the winter, start back again at Easter, you know? Usual thing."

"Somehow I thought you'd end up a Sunday School teacher . . . or a vicar."

Rachel laughs. "Oh I know. I was insufferable. I wanted to be like Sarah. I didn't want pictures and plastic sandals. I wanted a Bible with a zip around it and court shoes."

"So what happened? Did you convert to atheism?"

Rachel remembers a dream.

"I had this weird dream the other night. I was in this small tube; there was light shining through its walls, which were red and blue. I came up to this huge rock and I had to push it away but it was really heavy and I was struggling. And as I struggled I realised that I was actually outside one of the chambers of my own heart and I had to roll the stone away or I was going to die. You know like dad did . . . An embolism."

"Sounds like that film. Shit, what was it called? Where they shrank these scientists and then injected them into a vein. No! I know! Remember the numbskulls in the Beano? You're a numbskull. I always knew it."

"No! I am Lady Penelope! Will you let me finish? So . . . anyway, I roll back the stone and I enter this beautiful room. It's like a small temple. It's entirely lined with marble. And there are two basins in the shape of lotus flowers attached to the wall, and hot, steaming water is streaming over the top, and spilling onto the floor. Then – as my eyes grow accustomed to the dark – I begin to see more clearly and I can see that there is Jesus lying on a slab. I'm horrified because he's still wearing the crown of thorns and I know that I must help him. I carefully remove each thorn and bathe his wounds. Then I wash his body. And as I'm rubbing frankincense into his skin he wakes up, and he speaks to me. I can remember what he said. All of it. Word perfect."

"God you're weird. You haven't changed a bit. Okay then, tell me. What did Jesus say to you? Miss more-flakey-than-filo."

"He said: 'In the silent mind lies the master of life, within this stillness its mysteries are revealed. Seek to be still and know who you are, for beguiled by emotions we are blind.' Then he leans forward and pulls this bayonet out of my side. And I woke up."

"Jesus Christ! You ought to be in there with Mum. You were always having bad dreams. Nightmares. And sleepwalking. Drove us nuts."

"No I wasn't. When?"

"After Rebecca died. Mum and Dad used to take turns fetching you back from the mineshaft. You used to go up and sit next to it as if you were waiting for Rebecca to come back."

"Oh! My God. I never knew that. They never told me . . . "

"Sad really. God it was shit after that wasn't it?"

"I pushed her John. I pushed her. The barbed wire snapped."

John is still and quiet, staring at Rachel as if through a thick fog. She holds his gaze, notes his disbelief, his horror, his bewilderment.

"It was an accident. On my life it was an accident. I'd got angry. I pushed her . . . "

John leans forward and holds Rachel in his arms and lets her cry on his shoulder.

"I know how much you loved her. I know. We all did." He lets her cry a long time. "How come you're only just telling me?"

"I didn't know myself. I mean I didn't remember. I didn't remember until the day dad died. Somehow his death triggered the memory. I must have repressed it. I'm only just able to talk about it now.

It took so long to own it. I'm not sure I'll ever for-give myself. Not really."

"You know Rach, it could have been any of us. Supposing you'd drowned that day? I'd be the one sitting here confessing. Or the electric shock day? That might have killed you. I didn't think of any of this shit 'til we had Kaz. Then watching her grow up, and thinking of all the dangers – everywhere dangers. It did my head in. But we were wild. We'd be locked up now. Or Mum and Dad would be locked up and we'd all be in care."

"How come it has taken you over forty years to be nice to me?"

"Don't get used to it. This is an aberrant mo-ment. I need a drink. I need a big fucking drink. Let's go to the Tyacks."

"Thanks John."

"No, thank you."

"For what?"

"For being. Just for being."

They both sit for a moment and watch the sun-light glinting from the granite rubble of their small, ordinary lives.

"Actually," John continued, "thanks for not being Little Miss Perfect. You were such a shit at times."

Rachel slaps him very hard on his shoulder, and is deeply grateful for the resultant sting in her hand.

"You didn't answer my question. Are you a born-again atheist?"

"Not at all. I believe in something and I call it God. I think God and love are the same thing. Beyond that I don't understand any of that stuff. Trouble is religions are either divisive or exclusive."

Uncomfortable, John randomly changes the subject. "Hey! Do you remember The Singing Ringing Tree? Had a fish in it that always got frozen in a lake?"

Rachel laughs, flooded with sudden childish joy. "Yes! I do remember. It was brilliant."

John reaches in his pocket and pulls out a folded piece of paper and hands it over. "This is all I could find." He looks at Rachel as she carefully opens it and reads, and he wonders about her faith, wonders how she can live with what happened to Rebecca? What kind of God would allow a small child to plummet down a mineshaft?

"So Johnny Daylight died in 1958. He really did die. Abigail knew it. She knew it!"

"Sorry Sis you've lost me."

Rachel continues to read "He was a prospector . . . "

"What's it to you?"

"It's a very long story, I'll tell you about it sometime . . . It's funny though, for a while I thought I'd

260

end up like Abigail, but in fact I've really more in common with Johnny; we're both runaways . . . "

Perfectly Imperfect

Rachel walks through the crowded bar looking for John. She hasn't been in a bar for a long time and feels self-conscious and gauche. Bryan Adams belts out something about "cloud nine" from the jukebox.

Rachel is cursing John for abandoning her while he popped across the road to go to get cash from the cash machine. "Get the drinks in," he'd said, as if she'd been doing that forever. So she squeezes between two men and waits her turn at the bar.

"Hello." The man on her right wearing faded jeans and a blue and white chequered shirt is talking to her. He has brown eyes and a penetrating look.

"Hello. Sorry do I know you?"

"No. But I know you. You're Ruth Tangye's daughter."

Rachel has always been "Jack Tangye's daughter" and feels a sudden burst of pride. "Yes, I am. That's exactly who I am."

"I'm Glen Mortensen-Cave. I've noticed you visiting Ruth."

"I know you! You're an artist – a very fine one."

And just there, at that moment, they are each caught on the sharp point of romantic love, which, like grief, spins them around and around, until, before they know it, they are twisted, helplessly twisted, on its blade.

2005

Dear Abigail,

I don't know why I am not yet roaming the roads round here with my carrier bags. I have a selection stashed away somewhere, just in case the world crumbles and I give myself up to the Abigail inside me. Every time I visit my mother she is someone else; although the feisty Ruth still shines out from deep inside her. She finds it difficult to talk now, and doesn't appear to know who I am. But she is as loving as ever. And the staff at the home seem to adore her. We are having the longest, saddest goodbye.

I have given up my night-time strolls on the beach. Sometimes I get to snuggle up to the man who does not judge me, despite his artistic eye, which sees as well as looks, and his intimidating sense of aesthetic.

He – like you Abigail – helps me to face myself. And my small hope is that maybe I can do the same for him. It's Love.

And it's many other things . . .

Rachel xx

Hell's Mouth (2) 2006

The honeymoon couple are lying in the grass on the cliff top. They are tangled in each other's arms. He has his mouth buried in her neck and is blowing soft hot raspberries onto the skin just beneath her ear. It's driving her wild because he's found her weak spot – the place where pleasure and pain collide, one into the other. Her entire body is taut with anticipation; she thinks she'll die laughing. "I submit! I submit!"

He stops and they sit up, enjoying the easy silence that exists between them. It's a clear spring day, the sea is deep blue, almost navy, and, after yesterday's gales, surprisingly calm.

He turns towards his new bride and catches sight of a dark shape lying on the ground just to their right.

"What's that?" he asks.

"I don't know. Let's take a look."

They walk towards the black shape and it becomes apparent that it is an overcoat.

"Fancy leaving that behind," she says. "Look in the pockets – maybe there's some ID or something."

He pulls from one of the pockets a crumpled sheet of notepaper. He carefully straightens it out, and then silently reads to himself the letter scrawled on it.

Dearest Abigail,

My special man went back to his wife. I do not think he ever really left her.

Of course I would choose someone emotionally unavailable; no one knows more than you and I that like attracts like.

If only I could silence my mind . . . Sadly – like yours must have – it turns against me; it's a cancer . . .
Rachel xx

Steve looks at his darling wife Sarah and hugs her tight, thankful for their happiness.

Dream Girl

Carly Nugent

MPress books

For You

Doves fly over many streams of our future . . .
. . . Deep is the stream that the dove flies through . . .

Friday 1 November 2007, 7am

Alyson is at the top of an enormous waterfall. She is holding on to a rock for dear life, but the intensity of the water pounding down around her is so great that she can feel her grip loosening. She turns her head and sees a heavy chain – the sort that would anchor a large ship. The chain is wrapped around the rock she clings to and the other end bracelets her wrist. Alyson at once relaxes, knowing that this chain will surely save her from certain death at the foot of the falls. But then another Alyson is running up and down the riverbank, shouting, "The chain is holding you back! You must break the chain!"

Alyson's immediate reaction is to only hold tighter to the chain. But the small truth of the words rises steadily like a bubble in the water, and soon she is desperately flailing about, trying to release herself from the grip of the restraint. And as she does the chain grows heavier, until the other Alyson calls, "Let go!"

Alyson reaches an angry arm out from beneath the twisted sheet and slams her hand down hard on the alarm clock. She's tired; she feels as though she hardly slept. Somewhere in the ache of her muscles is a dream, but her mind floods with the press of her day.

Alyson is forty-eight and sleeps in a single bed, the same bed she slept in during her teenage years. In the same bedroom, in her parents' house. A bedroom kept dark with heavy brocade drapes, the colours of which have long since faded.

Alyson sits on the edge of the bed, her elbows on her knees, her head in her hands. This, her prayer position, this her mantra: get up Alyson. For God's sake, get up.

She sighs with resignation, stands up and, opening the curtains, floods the room with the morning light, which, like a photophobic, she turns straight away from. She wears pyjamas and covers these with a dressing gown, although it is not a cold house.

In the kitchen, she prepares a tray of tea and a mug

of hot water with a thick slice of lemon. Leaving the water behind, she picks up the tray and knocks on the living-room door. She enters without waiting for a response.

The light in here is being filtered through cream-coloured curtains, giving everything a bland softness. Yet this room looks more like a private room in a hospital than a homely lounge. The bed at its centre has an oxygen cylinder standing next to it, and some sort of machine hanging from the base beeps in time with a flashing red light, as air is pushed through a tube into the thick blue mattress. Pushed away in the corner is a large metal hoist, a sling hanging impotently from it, dangling dangerously close to a commode. Everything is clinically clean. And a large green wick pulled from a bottle fills the room with a pungent, citrine-chemical odour.

"Mum. Wake up Mum; it's time for your pills." Alyson takes a small key from her dressing-gown pocket and opens a bathroom cabinet, which has been fixed with a padlock. She efficiently dispenses pills into a tiny pot. Her mother has hardly stirred, but her lips have tightened. One eye has opened – and closed again.

It is from her mother that Alyson has inherited her good looks, but in repose, Alyson's face settles into a hard meanness. In fact, her entire being appears to be surrounded by an invisible electric fence, intuitively warning all those in close proximity to back away. Despite this, Alyson is blessed with the most captivating smile, it is an enchantment few are privy to. It greatly saddens her mother to witness all of her daughter's potential for joyful loving being thwarted by bitterness.

"Come on, Mum, you know I don't have time for this. It's Friday." Daniel's Day.

Alyson's mother, Esme, digs deeper into her pillowy dugout.

"Come on, Mum, you know I always win in the end. The day nurse will only give you an injection otherwise."

Esme's eyes spring open, but her hands are clenched into tight fists and a very careful observer would notice small wounds at her wrists, where, one night, she patiently sawed through her flesh with a blunt knife, saved from the tea tray. She might have succeeded in deeper, effective cuts had she not grown tired with the effort. In quiet moments she laughs about this. Laughs about futility. What does it teach – humility? She doesn't care anymore.

Alyson's father, Harold, whom she never married, but whom she lived in perpetual sinful loving with, would have discussed this endlessly with her. How she ached for him. Esme takes the pills and some of the tea into her mouth and in one violent effort spits them back into Alyson's face.

"Let me go!"

Unmoved, and without flinching, Alyson stands up. "Have it your own way." She leaves the room.

Satisfied, Esme returns to her dream of dying, content in the knowledge that the day nurse will not give her the injection, that she will do as she has always done: obey Esme's wishes and squirt it down the sink.

The dining room has been converted into a small gym. Friday might be Daniel's day but it is also weights day, resistance training. Alyson has the body of a woman half her age, but maintaining it comes at a price: two hours a day, six days a week. There's Yoga, Pilates, Taibo, Aerobics, weights, treadmill, rowing machine, trampoline and time on the sunbed. She shares none of these activities.

She used to run with Chris. It would always astonish her when they would return home breathless, and the first thing he'd do would be to light up a cigarette.

Alyson starts with the free weights, concentrating on the triceps and biceps. Since rotating and varying her training, her upper body strength has vastly improved, and the definition is good. But she is not satisfied yet. To her, her arms are still flabby.

When she first met Chris she was awed by his physique; it could not be described as 'a body', it was a piece of sculpture, hard as bronze. He belonged to a prestigious club, part of his 'works package'. At least that is what he said. Then again, he said a lot of things. To begin with, they only met on Sundays. It puzzled her later – and still does – why she was not more curious about this. Why did she so readily accept everything he said? But then, why would he lie? Why would anyone? He was a busy engineer, working on a major construction project that wasn't going to plan. And it was the eighties and interest rates were soaring and the property developers were becoming edgy. He kept on top of his work, but "Sundays are our day, babe."

That was nearly thirty years ago but his words still echoed in her head as if he had spoken them but a moment ago. As if the passage of time was irrelevant. She never really knew – and still doesn't – if he called her 'babe' to immediately gain some sort of authority over her and thereby subvert any she might have. Or did he simply do it because it was trendy? True, he was an unscrupulous, self-serving, manipulative bastard. But didn't that necessitate some ingenuity? Was he a genius or a fool? She will never know. And being with him . . . what had that made her?

Alyson shudders as she drives a flashback out of her head by lifting heavier weights. But it persists in full technicolour . . .

She's wearing a transparent black body; it has a high collar and long sleeves and the seams, at the crutch, are, deliberately, split open. Over the top is a black leather bustier, which must have cost a fortune. It zips up one side and there is lace at the front, for tying up – or not. She has fishnet stockings and her feet are squeezed into crippling, red patent, high heels that are a size too small. This detail she will take with her to her grave.

When Chris started to bring these things home, these gifts, ones that she could be more grateful about. She remonstrated about the heels; she was five feet eight, had been the tallest in her class, something she'd hated. And she hated the size of her feet more; she'd met men with smaller feet. Besides she had thick ankles. And fat thighs. How can anyone feel sexy when their thighs are oozing out of tight-stocking tops like toothpaste from a tube? All she felt was humiliation.

Of course, these 'gifts' didn't all come at once. Viewed now, all in all, it had taken a year, a small war of attrition.

"Why do you wash your make-up off when you come to bed?" There's a long pause. "I've never really understood why women do that. I mean, when they need it most, they take it off. It makes no sense. No sense at all, babe."

Alyson looks back at Chris; she is both shocked and dismayed and then hurt and dejected. He wants a doll, someone to dress up. A dream girl.

Chris had been experiencing difficulty achieving an erection. Initially, Alyson ascribed this to the copious amounts of red wine he drank, but he insisted it was more to do with her . . . After all, he "hadn't had this problem with anyone else . . ."

A counsellor friend had helpfully volunteered that Chris "was probably too close to his mother and therefore had to turn Alyson into a whore in order to fuck her".

It amazes Alyson now how she had leapt on this as a reason. How she had tried, armed with this newfound wisdom, to help him. How she had buried her head in the pillow. How she had worn the costumes he had bought for her. How she had let him flail about on top of her, getting angrier, redder and sweatier, before collapsing. He never came – not even close. It sickens Alyson to think of it, but he is a migraine she can't get rid of.

Chris's beautiful body had seemingly become flabby and flaccid overnight, his hard muscles giving way to flesh as soft as marshmallow. Alyson found out much later it was because he had given up the steroids. And of course it's all so easily explained when you have the truth. But the truth and Chris were on separate continents. He would stretch out on top of the bed, naked, his gross belly hiding his flacid penis.

He had an air of superiority, an arrogance that Alyson found mesmerising. "Come and get a load of this, babe. I'm the best thing that's ever happened to you."

He would stare at her, daring her to contradict his words. There was something in his eyes, some primal attitude that made her fearful, made her obey. Then he would get on top of her, almost suffocating her with his weight, and she'd try to help him; she would try to make his penis fit inside her. But it only folded like dough in her hands. And he would cover her mouth – with his Darren Nesbit lips – and somehow this intimacy was far, far worse. So she'd struggle away from him, moving her head, gasping for air, like someone having a panic attack.

Alyson shakes her head and tries to concentrate on lifting the dumbbells. If that had been the worst memory of their life together she might have been able to live with it, to move on, to become the person she was meant to be, the person that Esme and Harold had wanted her to be. But the anger and humiliation went to the core of her and so it became all she had from which to grow…

"Have you considered why you allowed him to debase you? Why you needed that in your life?" She hated Esme for saying this to her. Why had she confided in her oh-so-right-on-existentialist-CND-marching-and-bound-to-tell-her-father-fucked-up-mother?

Normal parents would have killed him . . .

The front door slams and the day nurse sings "good morning" to the hallway.

Grateful for the distraction, Alyson puts down the weights and meets the nurse in the kitchen.

"Mum needs her injection; she couldn't face the tablets. Although, I suppose we could crush them into her marmalade?"

"I'll see how we go. We may feel more co-operative after breakfast."

The nurse smiles enigmatically and this irritates Alyson. In fact there is something she cannot quite put her finger on about this particular nurse. She makes a mental note to get in touch with the agency and see if they can't find someone else, someone more . . . more . . . more . . . More? More intellectual.

Alyson goes upstairs to shower, running through all the things she wants to discuss with Daniel. Daniel would never lie to a woman. Why weren't all men blessed with his integrity?

For the first six months of her life with Chris, before he suddenly and unexpectedly announced that he would be moving in with her, he was actually a prisoner. He was not a 'busy engineer' but a drug smuggler. His 'free' Sundays were so that he might practice his religious observances with the Jehovah Witnesses. There were no provisions in his prison for JWs, so by way of meeting his religious needs and also his re-habilitation he was granted leave from 8am to 8pm each Sunday for the last six months of his three-year sentence.

Alyson found this out only much later, of course, during the inquest. (Naturally, he had lied about being a Jehovah Witness.)

She remembers sitting in the courtroom, Esme sitting next to her, unashamedly completing the Guardian crossword. Just as the coroner had said that Chris – or rather Mr. Christopher Matthews – had been a prisoner, Esme had solved a particularly tricky clue, and let out a very satisfied sigh, as if this detail explained everything. The coroner had nodded at her, in agreement, and Alyson had laughed – with shock and relief – because it did explain so much: the Sunday meetings, the fit body, the moving in. And the sex? Maybe. The lack of money. Certainly.

The very last thing Chris said to her was, "You haven't got the guts."

But she did have the guts.

Death by misadventure, that is what they called it. And ever since, Alyson had lived with the truth that she had murdered him and twice drove to the police station to confess to it, all the way in to the car park. Surely, she was much more useful 'outside' though, serving society, than she would be banged up? Besides, wasn't it a mercy killing, hadn't she saved the rest of the world from him? Hadn't she saved him from himself?

He was much better off dead.

She towels her body dry, has a good look in the full-length mirror, turns, and using a hand-held mirror, studies her rear. She's very, very happy with her body; a woman of her age should be proud. But when she steps forward and gets up close to her face, she is appalled by the stranger who stares back at her, the middle-aged glowering crone. This is the reason that builders on building sites still whistle and yell, and then stop as soon as she gets up close. This is the reason that young lads in boy-racer cars toot and slow down, only to then speed away, laughing. She feels that she is a disgusting parody of a woman. Is it possible to be narcissistic when you feel that your body is beautiful but your face is ugly? This is a question her parents would have discussed with their bohemian friends over long candlelit dinners that went on well into the night. The morning light bringing bodies on sofas, the acrid smell of stale cigarettes and exhaled alcohol, and Alyson shoved further away from her mum and dad, or rather, 'Esme' and 'Harold', by the intrusion of these strangers.

After living with her parents' closeness, with their utter devotion to each other, it was refreshing, in a way, to meet Chris. Chris, who only had time on Sundays. It was a day to look forward to. A sure thing. He always turned up. There were never any excuses. Those came later.

Alyson sometimes wonders who she would be now if she had never met Chris. Would she be affectionate and loving? Would she coil herself around Daniel and whisper 'I love you like no other' into his attentive ear?

With Chris, every day a truth became a lie or a lie became a truth. Every day of their three years together.

She lives with the damage he inflicted upon her as might a soldier live with a wound sustained in combat: hiding the physical and psychological harm from the enemy. The enemy being anyone within two feet of her and most especially, herself; after all, hasn't Esme always said, "You're your own worst enemy Alyson."

She slips into her freshly pressed dress and her polished low-heeled shoes and goes off to prepare for Daniel. She repeats his name like a loving mantra, rolling it around her tongue, swallowing it like a spoon of honey, Daniel, Dan-ie-l. Daniel Jennings. Mr. Daniel Jennings. He would be a man to dress up for in bed. He'd be someone you'd feel safe enough with to do that sort of thing. He'd be someone to split herself wide open for.

Alyson steps out into the sunshine and, for a small

moment, a smile softens and lifts her lips - and then disappears again, like a mermaid glimpsed in a treacherous sea.

Dream Girl

Carly Nugent

ISBN: 978-0-9565077-1-6